THE SOTH INITIATIVE

BOOK ONE

Dean Brior

ISBN 978-1-64471-973-2 (Paperback)
ISBN 978-1-64471-974-9 (Digital)

Covenant Books, Inc.
11661 Hwy 707
Murrells Inlet, SC 29576
www.covenantbooks.com

CHAPTER 1

The ground is hard, and the dust chokes his lungs, but he must run. The night is dark, and he stumbles on sharp rocks, but he must run. They have found him. He doesn't know how, but they have found him. He follows the path away from town, away from his family, and away from his son. His legs are strong, incredibly strong. All in his family had this strength, passed down from the man who was healed by Jesus. The story passed down to him by his family was just as the Bible had recorded. Jesus was teaching in a home that was packed with people. Some men wanted to bring a cripple to Jesus to be healed. They couldn't get through, so they climbed to the roof, cut a hole in it, and lowered the man down right in front of Jesus. Jesus smiled as he looked up at the faithful friends of this man. He looked intently at the man and said "Your sins are forgiven," but that wasn't enough for the Jewish leaders. Jesus showed his power as God by healing the weak, broken legs of this man.

His name was Johnathan and followed Jesus, even walking the way of the cross that fateful day. He lost his friend at the cross execution that weekend. For months, Johnathan was amazed at the strength his legs now had as a result of the healing. Not just strong, incredibly strong. He found a job carrying brick from the clay furnace to town, a hot, dusty five-mile walk he made many times a day. Most of his coworkers could make the difficult journey several times a day, but he did it ten times a day. At first, he walked as the others did, but soon he found that running with a sixty-pound sack didn't even cause him to sweat. Many watched in confusion and fear as this man healed by Jesus sprinted through his day. He had six children, four boys and two girls.

They all possessed the same strength in their legs and torso. They produced twenty children who also had the gift of strength. It seemed that the result of the healing was passed down somehow in the DNA of every family member until tonight. Tonight, the last relative of this family was running for his life. He had no children, and his family was that of a friend who had died suddenly two years earlier. He had taken them into his small home and cared for them as a father would. Now, he was running, praying they would not find the family and mistake them for his offspring. He was running wild, fast, incredibly fast, fueled by fear, angst, and hope—hope that he could out run the vehicle now careening over the dunes he was practically floating over. He caught the first bullet in the arm and didn't event slow for a moment.

The next bullet slammed into his shoulder, slowing for a moment, then back to a full sprint. The next three bullets landed in his lower back, and he went down hard. He was lying face down, his spine now shattered, his powerful legs hanging limp and useless, he blinked as he was rolled over and a light was flashed in his eyes. "Stupid animal, do you think you could out run us for the rest of your life? You are a corruption of nature, a freak who will die alone, weak, and powerless. After we finish with you, we will kill your family, tearing each leg out of its socket before we slit their throats. Allah be praised, you will not live to destroy our faith!"

The last thing he saw were the pins coming out of the two grenades he held and the look of horror as the attackers knew their lives would be forfeited tonight in the name of the cause. "The SOTH live!" he cried, "Jesus will be made known again!" Then the flash of death came over them all.

Philadelphia, Pennsylvania

Dr. Lyndon Johnson Batchelor, called Lindey by his friends, pushed the laptop away in frustration and confusion as he read yet another critique of his latest blog on the healing touch of Jesus Christ and the historical ramifications of it if Jesus was really God come down to man. As a professor of history and antiquities, Lindey was fascinated by the stories of all the healings that occurred in the Bible when Jesus walked and ministered to the people some two centuries ago. There had to be hundreds, maybe thousands, who experienced his touch during those three years of intense, world-changing ministry.

The events recorded in the four gospels contained reports of many kinds of healings done in many different ways. Some of them happened face-to-face as Jesus reached out and touched people who were healed instantly. Other healings occurred at a distance, with just a word or a thought from the travelling teacher of a new faith. Some occurred because of a person's faith, and others occurred in spite of their little faith. Some were healed as they cried out, and others were raised from the dead with no request made at all. Lindey struggled with the concept of miracle healings, but he was also drawn to the possibilities. His father had fought a valiant battle with leukemia, but had succumbed to the disease and passed away on a stormy night some eighteen months ago. His mother was brokenhearted to lose her partner of forty-five years, but she never questioned God or the reason her husband was called away at this time in their lives.

Lindey's older brother, Brock, a pastor of a growing church in Atlanta, performed the service and brought hope and strength to the attendees there that day—all except for Lindey and his younger sister Gwen. Gwen was an avowed atheist, walking away from the family faith when she graduated from GA Tech with a degree in engineering. She received no comfort from Brock's words, she just sat there, sad, lost, and feeling the pain of losing the one man she could always count on to love her with no strings attached.

Lindey listened to his brother's words, words about eternal life, an active and fulfilling place with the creator, and a future hope for all who put their hope in Jesus Christ. Lindey had embraced his father's faith like all of the family, learned the Bible from his youth, and determined to walk with God as he entered college, and started his life teaching others at the university.

Now, after crying out to God to heal his father, only to see him die in pain and suffering, Lindey was taking time out to consider this God of love. Did he really love that deeply? Was he really that concerned about his creation, or had he lost interest, allowed things to unwind, get out of hand, and slip into the morass that most of the world endured at this time in history. No, Brock's words fell on deaf ears for Lindey like they did for Gwen, but for very different reasons.

Qa'im, Iraq

The message had to be convincing but needed to be couched in enough mystery so as to allow for deniability in case she was discovered. Akifah was adept at computer hacking and knew this professor of history would not discover her ultimate plan until it was too late. She composed an e-mail that read:

> Please, Dr. Batchleor, travel to Lebanon Connecticut, to start your journey. You will meet an old man who will tell you of the history of the people Jesus healed. I have read your blog and can see your interest is genuine and born out of a passion for truth. Your truth journey starts in Lebanon, Connecticut, where you will meet Edgar Collingsworth. Ask him why he hides behind such an English name when his real name is Ariz Mohamad Aasad.

She pressed send and knew this was exactly what the professor needed to start his journey to find the leaders of the SOTH. Then she would be right there by his side, ready to kill them all. Akifah was a devoted Muslim and an elite agent and assassin who was part of the Cleansing Group out of Iran. She had been trained for espionage and murder since the age of 17, when she discovered the SOTH were involved in her family's mass extinction in a small town the SOTH had taken over in the early 1600s. She made a promise to their memory that she would find the leaders of the SOTH and wipe them out with Allah's vengeance. This American professor would be the lead she would follow all the way to the SOTH leaders.

Lindey eyed the e-mail with interest and doubt. Who would send such an e-mail and make it impossible for him to respond or even know who the sender was? He was interested enough to do a search of the town Lebanon, Connecticut, and of one of its elders, Edgar Collingsworth. The town had a modest beginning in 1700, where a group of families from England settled there, and lived for the most part, alone and sequestered behind large homes and larger walls formed by the connecting of each home at unique angles.

The Wikipedia report went on to reveal that this small town, today only 3500 strong, had produced seven governors, fifteen senators, and thirty-three state representatives, all related directly to the seven families that founded the town back in 1700. That was interesting, but there was more. Lebanon, Connecticut, enjoyed a rich and religious history as well, sending out hundreds of Christian missionaries, mainly to the Arab countries where that faith was not honored or even illegal in some places. Why so many leaders and servants in one small town, and who was Edgar Collingsworth? Once again, a few keystrokes later, and Lindey was looking at the handsome face of Edgar Collingsworth VII. This rendition of the Collingsworth clan was tall, fit, with fiery eyes that flashed of passion and love, even from just the digital rendition. He was a graduate of Oxford College in England, where he excelled in computer science at one of those DNA research companies.

He had been married for thirty-two years before losing his wife to an auto accident that left him paralyzed from the waist down. He moved back to Lebanon, Connecticut, ten years ago to serve as the town custodian, which was a position somewhat like a museum curator and historian all mixed together. Edgar VII fathered two children, both serving oversees in politics or in the government at very influential and powerful levels. The search did not reveal his home address, but it did show the address for the local office where he served four days a week. Lindey called his college employer and asked for a couple of days off to do some historic studies in a town in the Northeast. Five days later, he was on a train out of Philadelphia, PA, to Lebanon, Connecticut.

Akifah tracked the professor's keystrokes with deft talent born of necessity and hunger. She knew that understanding how to hack a personal computer and follow every action taken was something she needed to become an expert in, and she was. She saw the request for leave, the train ticket purchased online, even the hotel that Professor Batchleor was going to stay at, all neatly copied by the software program she had be trained on by certain members of the Cleansing Group, as they called their group.

It was more like a culture than a group. The Cleansing Group was created for one purpose only, to identify, track, and eliminate all families related to the sect of the healed, better known as the SOTH. The SOTH was formed after the people healed by Jesus began to experience an organized and deadly attack from several entities. Each person, who had received the healing touch of Jesus, was experiencing a residual effect, something that the supernatural experience left in their bodies. In fact, each person found they possessed certain physical, spiritual, and mental abilities they had not possessed before the encounter with Jesus. Each had also experienced the anger of the local Jewish synagogue where they were excommunicated and left with no communal support. Any person admitting to having been healed by Jesus was told to give glory to Jehovah and reject Jesus, or risk losing the opportunity to the Jewish support system they had known all their life. Many came forward and risked the shunning, as they told their stories, which were backed up by eyewitnesses.

The Jewish leaders were hopeful that by killing this renegade carpenter, and scattering his followers, they would end the movement like so many movements before had been ended. But this was not just another movement. Jesus had brought a message of love community, faith, and peace where the religious systems were bringing, well, religion. The people healed by Jesus had to be silenced, no matter what the cost.

Many of the healed came together after losing their place at the synagogue. They moved to small towns that did not seek to silence them. They lived out their lives in secrecy, but never between each other. They shared their stories often, with each other and their families. One of the leaders coined the name SOTH, standing for "sect of the healed." They knew God wanted them to do more than live in hiding, that he wanted them to be part of the fledgling movement that was being grown across the region by the apostles of Jesus. They began to connect with the apostles, asking to serve in the movement created by their newly found savior and healer, Jesus Christ. When the religious leaders scattered the apostles soon after Jesus's death, SOTH members moved with them, spreading their influence and families throughout the Roman Empire.

The Cleansing Group began to grow as well. Several religious leaders met with Roman leaders to squash the Jesus movement. They asked for the "Christ ones" leaders to be rounded up and prosecuted for blasphemy. Rome didn't care about petty Jewish squabbles, but they did care about maintaining order and control. The Jerusalem religious leaders caught on to this and painted a picture of social and political chaos if the movement was left unchecked. Some Roman leaders committed to work with some of the Jerusalem religious leaders and formed a pact dedicated to systematically wiping out all people who had experienced the healing touch of Jesus. This was the beginning of the Cleansing Group.

Today the group is larger, well-funded, extremely diverse, and unified around the total destruction of the SOTH relatives. It includes Muslims whose families experienced the power of SOTH members during the wars against the Jews and Christians in the first century. They see the SOTH as a direct threat to the Muslim faith, and the only choice they have is to kill the infidels whose DNA is an abomination to Allah. It contains nonreligious members who see this cultic group as a block to their plans to introduce a faith-free world based on man's intellect and self-determined force of will. There are leaders from the catholic and protestant faiths, threatened by any-thing not part of their own religious control and power structure. They see the SOTH as a potential challenge to the well-established religion of the time. There are members of the satanic church who believe the SOTH are destined to cause a great ingathering soon as they share the proof of their experience with the world.

This cannot happen in their eyes. There are even governments, the USA included, who want to capture and use SOTH members to fight against their opponents using this supernatural gifted population. This group, while never working together officially, have shared information and used each other throughout the centuries to achieve their goals of eradicating the planet from the SOTH at all costs.

Today, there are under one thousand SOTH members left in the world. They keep in touch by sophisticated software designed by some of the gifted members, and they are preparing to let the world know the realty of God and his son, Jesus. They possess certain artifacts that have been hidden and held in preparation for the time God revealed they should be shared with the world. Things such as the nails used at the cross, the cup and plate Jesus used at the last supper, even the many Jewish treasures, including the Ark of the Covenant, protected all this time by Templar families. Yes, the world would see, the world would believe, and the world would return to the God who loves them enough to die and rise again for them.

CHAPTER 2

CIA headquarters, McLean, VA

Garrett Barkley, a ten-year veteran of the CIA, signed on to his highly encrypted laptop, and waited the three minutes it took to establish and confirm his identity and the security of his connection. So much of technology was open to attack, originating from hackers who maintained a sort of control over thousands of personal computers the general public was ignorant to. Garret also participated in this hacker culture, and he was paid well by the government to do it.

He checked into a particular laptop he had been tracking for two weeks. The "client" was a Professor Batchelor, who had been writing a blog on the historical significance of the healings of Jesus. He had created some interest from some national and international entities Garret was familiar with, and he was interested to see where this lead went. Garret was assigned to an elite team of cyber hackers who had tracked, identified, and listed close to a hundred unique individuals over the past three years. They called themselves the sect of the healed or the SOTH. Garret wasn't much of a religious person, and he didn't believe in miracles, but the group he studied possessed special gifts and talents he could not easily explain.

His superiors had only shared that they wanted the people on the list to be tracked and kept available to be brought in at any time. That was an easy task as the civilians on the list had no chance of avoiding the Transparent Target software that he had been using to keep tabs on them all. Originally developed by the DOD as a means of finding and tracking terrorists on the run, this software loaded a parallel virus file that opened the user's computer to the tracker with no chance of ever being discovered. Keystrokes were analyzed and coded into easy to read reports. Garret knew when his targets slept, what they ate, where they went, and how much they spent every day of their lives.

He could event ping their phone and know their location at any time, even when the phone was shut down. This level of invasion was reserved for only the highest terrorist target, so why did they have him using it on ordinary citizens? Garret didn't care, he was a man who obeyed orders and excelled in his craft. After five years in the program, two spent in training and the last three tracking SOTH members, he had grown weary of the daily grind and was contemplating a move in the near future.

Huh, that was funny, Garret thought to himself as he read the past days report on Dr. Batchleor. A last-minute request for leave, along with a train ticket to someplace called Lebanon, Connecticut. A quick online search gave him on information to answer his question of why the last-minute trip. Garret would be there with his team to record and download every moment. The new upgrade to Transparent Target was a patch that would allow a person to listen to all incoming sound and speech from a thirty-foot radius around a target's phone, laptop, or iPad. The software could filter out each sound and give the listener clear access to each person speaking, or listen to surrounding sounds, even the keystroke sounds of a nearby computer. Dr. Batchleor was scheduled to leave his home tomorrow morning and arrive in Lebanon, Connecticut, by 9:00 a.m. Garret and his team would be there—listening, recording, and looking to understand what the professor was up to.

Lindey had packed quickly, gathering just the essentials for his overnight excursion to Lebanon, Connecticut. His searching for more information on Edgar Collingsworth was unfruitful as the man was strangely absent from most online media and social search engines. His academic pursuits were listed—graduating top of his class at Oxford in 1973, then on to a doctorate on genetics and DNA sequencing. His place of employment out of college was with a start-up computer software company, where he rocketed to the top of his profession. In 1997, he was lured away by another fledgling company that was getting involved in the DNA sampling market and told him they wanted his genius in computing as well as his degree in DNA sequencing. Regenerate, LLC, was a small English firm that did DNA reports for people as they would send in their saliva samples to be loaded and compared to millions of other samples.

The promise was to tell a person what their actual heritage was based on a worldwide algorithm gleaned from the millions of samples that poured in from people fascinated with the technology. Little did the public know that the software was also used to catalog, and file people based on ethnicity, blood type, disease tenancies, and even longevity based on DNA structure and study. Less people knew about the real purpose of Regenerate, LLC, currently located on the Thames River five miles out of London.

They advertised as one of hundreds of DNA study companies, and they did provide that service, along with other more nefarious services that would not be fully appreciated by the paying public. The software Edgar Collingsworth was responsible for was designed to categorize people based on specific DNA markers. Edgar could access every DNA report company at will, inserting a virus that would search for specific markers, and report the person's information back to him in a daily report. He would know their name, address, health, banking habits, where they worked, and who they were related to. It was the last nugget, who they were related to, which Edgar was most interested in. He would use this information to connect with the other surviving family members of the SOTH.

Edgar was a direct descendant of Ameel, a little boy healed by Jesus shortly before his crucifixion. He traced his DNA to that of his ancient relative down to the last marker. This is why he worked at Regenerate, LLC. He was using the software to find and identify people with unique DNA markers, possibly those of the relatives of other people healed by Jesus. He had sifted through hundreds of thousands of samples, using an algorithm designed by him to find others like him. He had found 385 people over the past 5 years.

Contacting them proved to be a challenge as they all seemed to know they were being sought after, and they would slip into hiding and go off the grid, making locating them nearly impossible. *Nearly* impossible because Edgar had developed the ability to connect with people in a way that was most impressive. In time, he developed trust with the SOTH, even becoming part of their leadership, and protecting them with his technological talents. His mission was to find, protect, and prepare the SOTH for the great revealing.

One rainy day, Edgar was caught by his superiors using his private software on company property. They not only fired him, but threatened bodily harm if he were to ever come back to England. He was given two one-way plane tickets and asked to leave that evening. He hurried home and explained to his wife why they had to flee. She had known of these special abilities and had encouraged him to carry on with his efforts to find the SOTH members who were left in the world. Now, they were on their way to the airport, speeding along the coast as the storm increased in fury. Out of nowhere, a large van appeared, high beams blazing, and careening into their lane. Edgar instinctively swerved to the left, plummeting down a hundred-foot embankment that terminated in a large bolder field.

When he awoke, he was staring at a hospital monitor that was tracking the rhythmic beat of his heart. The reading increased quickly as he thought about his wife. He was informed that she had died in the crash and that he had severed his spine in the accident. He thought of reporting the van and his suspicion that Regenerate was behind it, but he knew better. In time, he healed and returned to Lebanon, Connecticut, serving the community, and searching, always searching for the SOTH.

Lindey used the three-hour commute by train to further his study of Lebanon, Connecticut's history. The original seven families that founded the small-town October 10, 1740, had all come from England, but all of the men were of Jewish decent. Lindey thought it strange that all the men were Jewish, while all the women were of English descent. For the first twenty years, the town remained secluded and unfriendly to outsiders. Soon, the seven families raised over 50 children who gave them over 125 grandchildren by the time the town was established forty years. When the war for independence arrived in 1776, the Lebanon, Connecticut, community served proudly by sending many of their men to serve in the newly created local, state, regional, and national houses of representatives.

Several went on to serve with distinction as generals and aids to generals during the war to break away from England. Lindey found that no less than seven governors, fifteen state senators, and five national senators, as well as many lower level political positions were held by families from Lebanon, Connecticut. What was the reason that so many professional and public servant people came from this one small town?

Lindey stepped off the train into a brilliant fall day. Lebanon, Connecticut, was a twenty-minute Uber ride from the station, and with every turn, Lindey was delivered into a beautiful landscape of forest, babbling brooks, and peaceful serenity. Lindey arrived at the small town, which had grudgingly developed into a quaint tourist town, complete with a central park and large and circular gazebo that looked like something right out of an old time Andy Griffith show. He was staying at the local bed and breakfast, but only stopped to drop off his things. It was 3:30 p.m., and he knew the hours of operation for the town historic office was nine to five that day. He walked the half a mile distance to the office, which was attached to the local constable office. He knocked on the door and entered to find Edgar Collingsworth sitting amidst piles of documents and files. He knew the man he was looking at was Collingsworth, you couldn't miss those blazing blue eyes complimented by his broad smile of perfect teeth.

"Mr. Collingsworth?" Lindey asked, to which the man replied, "Ed will do Professor Batchleor."

Lindey was confused as he had just left a message this morning that he would be stopping in to talk about the town history today around 4:00 p.m.

"Sorry, Professor, I like to do some investigation on my visitors, that's how I knew your face when you came in. Please, come into my office."

"You can call me Lindey, Ed, since you seem to know a lot about me already"

"I hope you aren't offended by my need to do some digging on you, Lindey. I just like to be prepared to assure that I will be able to help you the best I can."

"No," Lindey said as Ed ushered him past the messy desk into another room, this one larger and more orderly.

"I'm afraid my assistant, Jennie, is a little behind her work. We should be able to meet here in the museum."

It was then that he noticed they were entering a large, rectangular room with historic artifacts stored behind glass shelves and display tables. Everything from the independence war to the civil war to everything after that was carefully housed in this small but impactful museum.

"I see your area of study at the university is American history, with an emphasis on the influence other countries have had on the development of government and social structures. I also enjoyed reading your blog on the historic significance of people related to those healed by Jesus of Nazareth."

Lindey was on guard now, he hadn't been prepared for Ed's deep dive into his online presence. He wondered if Ed was suspicious of Lindey's motives for coming today.

"Yes, I've been having a conversation with interested people all over the world who would jump at the chance to meet a relative of a person healed by Jesus. The historic significance of finding a person like this would be a direct window into the past, and a chance to interview them to find out if they had 'kept the faith' as it is. I'm a little befuddled by the fact that no sign of those relatives seems to exist anymore. It's as if every family involved in a Jesus healing has disappeared after all these years"

"I'm curious as to why you would come to Lebanon, Connecticut, to start your search. We are a sleepy tourist town with a long history of simple people living simple lives."

Lindey decided to jump right in and gauge the man's reaction to the information he had.

"In fact, Ed, one of those bloggers e-mailed me with your name, and asked me about what they said was your real name, Ariz Mohamad Aasad."

Edgar Collingsworth looked back with just a slight tremor in his cheek muscle, revealing that the name did hold some significance to him.

"Ariz Mohamad Aasad, is that the name you were given? Who gave you this name, Lindey? Why are you really here?" Ed had wheeled his chair to a large, antique desk that looked like it was both three hundred years old and just built last week.

Lindey sat in an old high back chair, the kind that had wings coming from the top of the furniture. "Mr. Collingsworth, I am just following up on a lead from an anonymous source, and I wanted to confirm if indeed there had been relatives of people healed by Jesus living in Lebanon, Connecticut. I know many of the founding fathers were men of Jewish decent, and I am impressed by the amount of professional and political men and women who have come out of this town. You moved back about ten years ago, correct?" Lindey was trying to diffuse the tension he felt arising from the revelation of the name Ariz Mohamad Aasad. Maybe asking for Ed's own personal history would get the conversation going again.

"Yes, I came back after losing my wife in an auto accident in England where we lived."

"I'm sorry for your loss Ed. You graduated from Oxford with a degree in DNA sequencing, am I right?" Lindey asked.

"Yes, that is correct. I came back to retire in my hometown and help out with the town museum in my spare time. I'm afraid I'm baffled by the mysterious blogger who thinks I am somebody else. I've never heard that name before, and it doesn't sound familiar as a name that would be found in the history of Lebanon, Connecticut."

There it was, a simple denial with a measured response. Lindey didn't know what to do with that answer, so he continued his historical questions.

"Lebanon, Connecticut, why choose such a foreign name for a town born out of English puritan families?"

"As you obviously know, only the founding women were English, their husbands were refugees of the Jewish purging by Muslim armies in the late 1600s." Ed was speaking formally now, as one who was on guard and moving away from a friendly demeanor. "They migrated to England, found wives to marry, and came across to start a new live with their English wives. The result has become the beautiful town you see around you today. They did want to remember their Arabic history by naming the town after their home country. It is true that many of our citizens have served in both professional and political arenas, but that would be true for many of the towns that were started in the 1700s."

Lindey stammered for a moment as he began to piece the picture he was getting in his mind. It was almost like he was receiving some message from an unknown source. He blurted out, "So when did you realize you were a descendant of a healed person, Ed?"

Ed looked down, sighed, and then looked up, those blazing blue eyes looking intense, so intense Lindey looked away in self-awareness that he had crossed a line in the conversation. He then felt a strange, pressing on his skull, almost like somebody was standing behind him, turning the crank on a vice. He looked back to Edgar, and saw that his gaze had not changed, but his eyes were almost on fire with color and light. Lindey began to get dizzy, and the last thing he saw was the painting of the town gazebo on the wall he was now glancing up at.

CHAPTER 3

Garret had arrived in Lebanon, Connecticut, in the "company van" along with three agents supplying technical and physical backup. His tracer had Lindey at a local bed and breakfast where he stayed for the evening. His superiors had sent him on a recognizance mission, to gather information and identify any contacts Lindey may meet with while in the town. Just before he left from DC, Garret was sent an anonymous e-mail telling him to find and interrogate an Edgar Collingsworth living in Lebanon, Connecticut.

This was strange to be receiving an e-mail directing him to the one place he was secretly headed to that afternoon. He did a backstop trace on the e-mail, which ended in a cyber café in London. He called CIA agents there and had them hurry to the café, finding nothing significant. He did a quick download on an Edgar Collingsworth and found that he was on a CIA watch list from the England office.

They knew he was living in Lebanon, Connecticut, but they were biding their time, not even sending a surveillance team to the town. Something about working at a DNA company and doing extensive and illegal cyber hacking into all of the DNA servicing companies in Europe. Protocol called for Garret to contact the London office and let them know he was entering their turf, even if for an unrelated reason. Garret decided to hold off for now and see if the two targets connected with each other. Targets? Did he just consider these innocent Americans targets? The classification of a target was much more serious than just a surveillance "client" as Garret like to call them. Then he remembered that the upper level people he served had coined the phrase to him just that morning as they sent him off to "spy" on Dr. Batchleor.

Lindey woke up as the morning light shown on his bed. He was reeling from a massive headache that reached into his upper back. He felt disoriented, stunned as if from a taser, although he had never been tasered. He couldn't remember where he was or why he was there. His mind was clouded, like a cover had been brought down on his conciseness. He sat up and took several minutes to gain a sense of balance and awareness. What was this room, and why was he here? The smell of hot bread baking wafted up to his room, and he took it in with delight. That smell brought him back to his childhood, when Mom would greet him from a long day at play with her homemade bread and biscuits. He closed his eyes and returned to that simple and blessed time, a time when there was a joy to every moment, and the family was whole, healthy, and happy.

Then his mind snapped to attention. He was in Lebanon, Connecticut, looking for, looking for, what was the name? Ed. Edward, Edith, no Edgar, Edgar Collingsworth. Now he remembered. He was interviewing Edgar, he mentioned his suspicion that Edgar was part of the family of a healed person, then the lights went out. It took him several more minutes to orient himself, and carefully navigate the stairs to the lobby.

Now, he walked out into the brilliant morning sunshine and surveyed his surroundings. All was quiet, quaint, and suspicious. He rushed over to the museum, only to find it locked and abandoned. He moved next door and found the constable at his desk working on his computer. "Excuse me, but do you know where Edgar went?"

The man looked up and answered with his own question, "Edgar Collingsworth?"

Jerusalem, 34 AD

"Why do you persecute us, sir, we have done nothing to you." The cries of the woman came from behind an old, wooden door, not meant to keep invaders out, and certainly not strong enough to stop a Roman soldier and his command from coming in. "Open this door, slave, or we will break it in half."

She opened the door, and five large, armed soldiers filled the tiny common space the family used as a living room, kitchen and bedroom. "Is this the family of Samuel, the butcher who claims his son was healed by the blasphemer Jesus of Nazareth?" Leah had been preparing for this time, but it came so abruptly she hadn't been ready.

Samuel had laid his son, Ameel, on the path Jesus was taking to Jerusalem. People said he was healing hundreds of people, from physical illness to demonic captivity. Samuel was hoping for his own miracle, one the local religious leaders could not help him with. His son was mute and had not uttered a word since he was born. Neighbors saw this as a judgment from God as they saw all illness and suffering. Earlier that week, Samuel had watched as Jesus had an encounter with the local leaders of the synagogue. They brought a man born blind to him, asking, "Who sinned that this man was born blind?"

Samuel watched as Jesus walked up to the man and looked deeply into his eyes. The man shuddered and groaned, his eyes fluttering under his lids in spasms, then calming as he opened his eyelids with a gasp. The first thing the man saw was his healer, to which he dropped to his knees and cried, "Thank you, Lord, thank you, thank you thank you."

Jesus looked at the leaders and said, "Nobody has sinned to cause this blindness, it was allowed so that you could see the works of God amongst you and believe."

Then Samuel watched as Jesus and his apostles walked away, leaving the leaders speechless and still blind to their own sin.

Samuel knew that if he could just get his son near Jesus, he would speak like all of his siblings. The day came when he saw the great crowds of people following Jesus as he began his journey to Jerusalem. There was only one road in the area that led to the capitol, and Samuel was waiting right on the side of the road when Jesus came by. So were hundreds of others, pushing and shoving, fighting to get their chance at a healing or miracle. Samuel lost sight of his son in the crowd, but found him standing in front of Jesus, the prophet's hand resting on his head. They were talking to each other, like it was a normal thing to do.

Some of his neighbors were there, but they didn't believe it was Samuel, the butcher's son. Now Samuel had reached his son, and Jesus was moving on. He turned as Samuel reached his son and lifted him up with joy and celebration. "Abba, Abba, Jesus made me speak!"

Jesus looked back and smiled, a smile of pure joy at the sight of a laughing and giggling son embraced by his father.

Now, they were hunting for him, both father and son. The Romans had begun to round up all the people associated in any way to the recently crucified carpenter of Nazareth. They had been reported by a neighbor, and they weren't going to leave without father and son. By some miracle, Samuel and Ameel had worked late in the fields and saw the soldiers pushing through the doorway. "Wait here, Son, and go to your uncle's house the next town over if you see me taken away by the soldiers. Trust in Jesus your healer, you are his son now." The father plunged into the house where there began a loud and defiant struggle.

Amidst screams from his mother and tears from his sisters and brothers, Ameel cried as he watched three soldiers drag his father to a wagon and strap him down. One soldier went to the back of the house, and another covered the front entrance in case the son returned in the night. It was the last time he would see his family. Ameel cried and heaved until he could cry no more. He made it to the house of his uncle and lived out his life there. He had five children, all possessed a remarkable ability to communicate truth and lead people with their words. Generation after generation showed the residual effects of the first healing, including the man who would move to London and help found the small town of Lebanon, Connecticut, Ameel Azir.

He changed his name to Randolph Collingsworth, met a godly English woman with money and a yearning for religious freedom offered in the new world of America. Generations would pass until another relative would take over the family mantle. His father named him Ariz Mohamad Aasad, but his American name was Edgar Collingsworth, of the Collingsworth clan, one of seven families who escaped the Cleansing Group and started their new lives in America.

Lindey was frustrated but cautious in responding to the constable's words. He needed to find Edgar, not drive his chances away with an angry retort. "I'm sorry, doesn't Edgar Collingsworth work next door and the museum?"

"Yes, sir, but he has been out of town for over a week now. Something about going back to England on business."

"What?!" Lindey cried out, losing his composure anyway. "I spent two hours yesterday at this place, and I demand to see Edgar Collingsworth!"

"Sir, I'd like to help you," the man said with no passion or conviction, "we have a college intern who works there a couple of days a week, but she is out for the week and was not here yesterday. Are you sure you were at this address yesterday? I was out as well, but you must have mistaken this building for another."

He returned to his computer screen, dismissing the confused tourist who he assumed had been nursing a hangover from the looks of him. Lindey couldn't stand the stonewalling, but he knew this was a dead end. He stormed out of the constable's office and stopped to look into the window of the museum. It was swept clean, not one piece of paper on the old desk that only yesterday held mountains of documents. He knew a whitewash when he saw one, and he knew he would not find any information about Edgar Collingsworth in Lebanon, Connecticut.

Garret watched, and recorded, as Lindey ran out of the bed and breakfast into the local constable's office. Minutes later, he stormed out and ran to the bed and breakfast. He was out the door in five minutes, carrying a small overnight bag. He was on his way to the train station and home to his books and office. What had happened here? Who did Lindey meet? Why was he leaving so abruptly? Garret watched an hour later as Lindey boarded the train for home. He told his team to wrap up the site and head home as well.

He had contemplated visiting the constable's office, flashing his badge, and getting as much information as possible form the man on why Lindey had come here. He decided against it as he was instructed to operate in the background at all times, no exposure to the public or local law officers for any reason.

Qi'am, Iraq

Akifah also watched the professor from her digital vantage point as Lindey left Lebanon, Connecticut. He had gotten what she wanted, the location of the record keeper of the SOTH, the man who had discovered the DNA algorithm to find and track SOTH members across the world. Now, she would track and capture this mutant infidel, torturing him for his knowledge and then torturing him for his part in the slaughter of her family.

Lindey checked his messages on the train ride home His mother had left him one of her typical messages; "Lindey, this is your mother, the one who gave you life. Where are you son, why don't you return my calls? If you know what's good for you, you'll call me immediately. I know where you live, and I'm not afraid to come up there and embarrass you with a song and dance right on your front lawn. Love you, Lindey, and call me!" The voice mail ended.

This was her way with her middle son. They had similar personalities, but never allowed that to create tension like it normally did with a parent and a son. Elizabeth loved her children fiercely, and they all knew it. Even her daughter knew she was loved, despite the fact that she had walked away from her faith while attending college. Lizzy girl, as Lindey's father called her, had a simple faith that was deep and solid, no matter what the world threw at her. Her husband, Richard's, death had rocked her world, but her belief that he would be waiting for her in heaven had allowed her to move through the grieving process with strength and poise.

Her children handled his passing in their own ways. Lindey was still processing the whole thing, including the last year of his life when, in spite of his prayers, his father suffered immeasurable pain as his body submitted to the cancer's invasion. "Just take him, God," was one of his often-mentioned prayers. Why did such a good man have to suffer so much? All his life, he was a servant and leader. He served and loved his family, he served and loved the employees of his cleaning and recovery business, and he served and loved the people at the church he helped found thirty years ago. Ricko, his nickname coined by his bride, had a joy and happiness that even cancer couldn't kill. His amiable nature and quiet way of engaging people made him a favorite patient on the cancer treatment floor.

Several nurses and two orderlies had started attending church as a result of Ricko's influence. Lindey was proud of his dad and loved his way of always finding the humor in a situation.

Now, Lindey was wondering if God was even there the last year of his dad's life. He doubted God, maybe for the first time in his life. It was more than doubt, it was anger too. If God loved Richard Batchelor, why did he allow him to suffer so much at the end of his life? Yes, Lindey was angry, but not with a hatred anger. It was more like a deeply disappointed anger, a slow burning ember that would flare up at the most unlikely times. Now, that anger was on a slow boil as he tried to remember his conversation with Edgar Collingsworth. What did Edgar do to him? Why did he only remember pieces of the encounter? Did Edgar drug him? Slip him an aerosol mickey fin? Or was it his eyes, those powerful, riveting eyes, blazing with blue fire, almost reaching out to him, reaching out, then assaulting him!

Yes, that was it. Edgar possessed some kind of mental telepathy that could affect a person's mind to the extent of rendering them unconscious and even causing some kind of short-term amnesia. Edgar was one of the relatives of a Jesus-healed person, that was certain. Could this be the residual effect he had heard about before and written about in his blog? Why did Edgar react so strongly to Lindey's questions? What did he want to keep hidden? Too many questions with not enough answers. For now, Lindey would return home, call his mother, tell her nothing about his adventure in Connecticut, take a hand full of aspirin, and sleep off his encounter with Edgar.

Edgar's office in Lebanon, CT

Edgar caught Lindey gently as he slumped to the floor. He disliked using his "influence" on other people, but this man has so quickly and easily uncovered his identity, that he reacted with knee jerk fear and almost deadly focus. Edgar had realized his "gift of persuasion" as a young boy. While being bullied, he thought about how he wished the boy hurling insults at him would get sick and go away.

In a moment, the bully's eyes went up into his head, and he spewed a raw concoction of digested lunch and milk all over himself and those nearby.

The boy was sick for two days, and Eddie was fearful of what he caused to happen. When he shared this with his father, he told Eddie that he should only think nice things about people and never see them getting hurt in his mind's eye. Eddie obeyed his father, and soon became one of the most popular students in the school. He discovered that if he thought pleasant thoughts about his classmates, even his teachers, they would be drawn to him, even the bullies, and they would follow him if he needed them to. He used this influence for good and created a kind environment in his school that made his father proud.

When he was twelve, he had another brief encounter that rocked his world. He got in a fight with a boy who was jealous of Edgar's friendship with a girl the boy liked. As the boy pushed him and called him names, getting ready to physically harm him, he focused on the boy's eyes. Suddenly, the boy stopped talking and looked around him. "What happened, why can't I see, what did you do to me you, freak?"

Some of the students has begun talking about Eddie's abilities, and some of them were scared of his "gift." Eddie released the boy and ran home to confess his sins to his father that evening. "Eddie, it is time you knew the truth about your gift. You are a descendant of the SOTH, the sect of the healed, the people Jesus Christ healed while he was on the earth."

Eddie knew Jesus, he had followed in his father's faith and knew the Bible fairly well, even at his age. "Which one, Dad, which one?" Eddie asked with excitement.

"It was not a person in the Bible, my son, it was a godly man named Samuel who brought his mute son to Jesus on the road to Jerusalem."

His son was also called Ameel, and he was separated from his family when the Roman soldiers came to take him and his father away for being connected to Jesus. Ameel had the gift of the spoken word after that and the ability to convince people of truth.

You have that same gift, Eddie, but your gift has manifested into a cognitive power, one that can influence others to the level you experienced today at school. I have been waiting for this day and praying for God to show me the path he has for you. This gift is from God, passed down from generation to generation, Eddie. We must honor God with the use of this gift, and resist using it in ways that would hurt people, or bring attention to us in any way. There are people in the world who would want to harm us, Eddie, people who don't understand who we really are. You must commit to disciplining your emotions to keep from ever using your gift in a negative way again.

Edgar had only gone back on that commitment twice since the day his father confronted him. Once as he dealt with the men who killed his wife and paralyzed him, and yesterday when his secret was exposed by a professor of history. He knew the town would cover for him, erasing every proof of his existence using the software program Edgar had developed for himself and other SOTH members who needed to disappear quickly from their pursuers. As Edgar relayed his situation to the other SOTH members, Sarah, the SOTH leader at the time, suggested a meeting to move up the time frame for the great revealing. "We need to coordinate with the European and Asian teams in order to have all of the proof texts and artifacts gathered together in one place for maximum effect."

Edgar agreed but warned them all that the cleansing group was catching up to them, as he related the recent death of a SOTH member in Lebanon last week and the need for four families to "disappear" with his help. Now with the exposure in Lebanon, Connecticut, more people would be at risk from the growing tentacles of the Cleansing Group. "God is telling us to make it plain that he does exist, he is real, and he is ready to welcome any person into his everlasting arms of love. The world has grown cold and calculating, losing the ability to see truth event truth that has lasted two thousand years. Now is the time to show the SOTH collection of biblical proof, and watch the world come back to its creator."

"My algorithm found six more potential SOTH leads, and I am working on their location even now."

Sarah responded; "I'm glad we are still finding remnants of our family, but I need to speak to you about this professor Batchelor. God has given me a very direct idea about him. "He must find us, Edgar, trust me on that. We must go to Naples to the place of safety and prepare for the great revealing."

CHAPTER 4

Arqa, Lebanon

Mohamed awoke to the morning call to worship, one of five times he would stop and bow toward his beloved Mecca today. He was filled with awe and foreboding as he opened his laptop and reread the e-mail that was anonymous and impossible to trace. It said, "You will have a visitor soon who will need your expertise on the family history of Emperor Alexander Severus. He will ask about the healed ones, and you are to answer his questions. I will be there as well, acting as interpreter for him. He will not know that I am your ally, the one who will use him to uncover the healed ones and wipe them off the earth in Allah's name. You are a relative of my employer, sworn to protect the secret of the Cleansing Group. You will use this man to find the ones hiding amongst us, and he will die with them when their time comes."

Mohamed knew who this was now, this was Akifah, known to westerners as Sophie Johnson, the black widow spy who had tentacles into every town where the SOTH were said to inhabit. There was a small force of highly trained men and women who were at her disposal, and people who did not follow her orders ended up dead, or never found again.

She was connected at the highest levels of governments across the world and could make a person disappear off the face of the earth, no digital or virtual footprint left. She had done this hundreds, maybe thousands of times, and now she was coming to his town. Mohamed sighed, rolled out his prayer mat, and faced toward mecca. He was not a violent man, and did not relish the violence as so many of his relatives did. He felt bad for this ignorant American walking into a certain death trap. But he knew that Allah needed him to rid the world of the filthy mutant SOTH, and he was committed to that cause. He would meet the foreign infidel and show him how powerful Allah was.

Frederick, Maryland

Lindey once again pondered the meaning of the e-mail that had just popped up on his screen. "Your journey is not over, Professor. Do a search on a small town in Lebanon called Arqa. You will find what the old man doesn't want you to find there. Go to Arqa, and learn about the emperor Severus, or, shall I say, learn about his heritage. You will begin to understand why the people of the healed ones stay in hiding, and cower in their homes."

Arqa, Lebanon, was a Sunni-run village near the shores of Lebanon—twenty-two kilometers form Tripoli. It had seen all of the world religions pass through and control its people, from Rome to Catholics to Islam, which it was today. It is currently a Sunni controlled town. The Sunni faith sees itself as the orthodox faith of Mohamed, the traditional teachings being passed down to the largest faith in the world.

They broke away from the Shiites, naming Abu Bakar as their first Caliph, or spiritual leader. Most people do not know that these two sects are responsible for most of the Muslim deaths and terrorism activity in the world. Although serving Allah the same, they differ as to who is in authority, and who is the leader of the future of the Islamic faith. Sunni follow Sharia law, which can be cruel and unforgiving to women, children, and any man crossing their path. Death squads regularly visited small towns like Arqa, and "justice" was carried out in public to make sure the people saw the outcome of practicing any other form of Islam but theirs.

Arqa was also home to the SOTH. This is where a group of the healed by Jesus wandered to as the Christian faith began to spread out under Roman persecution. Years before, a Roman soldier, Braccus, came to Jesus and asked for his servant to be healed. Jesus said he would come to the man's house, but Braccus said he was not worthy of Jesus entering his house. Jesus could just give the word, and he believed his servant would be healed.

Jesus was impressed by this non-Jew's faith and said that it would be done according to his faith. Braccus returned to see his Jewish servant, Areaneus, fully restored to health. Braccus became an ally to the Christian faith, protecting and hiding many of the SOTH from the cleansing group that was forming and growing in numbers. Areaneus the servant who was healed, became a trusted advisor, exhibiting an uncanny ability to understand people and their tendencies. The two became close friends even after the soldier became a centurion in his later years. Their children grew up together, and the Roman government gave Areaneus his citizenship based on the Braccus's letters and monetary gifts to the government.

They moved to Arqa when Braccus was reassigned to what was now known as Caesarea Arqa, as it was under Roman rule. Many years later, Areanus's family would produce an exceptional leader named Alexander Serverus, who became an emperor to Rome. Alexander used his influence to open doors for the Christian faith to flourish and allowed churches to exist where he could. He was a SOTH relative and used his power to better the kingdom of God. Once discovered by the cleansing group, he was assassinated by them and replaced with a more ardent supporter of the cleansing group, Emperor Thrax.

Lindey knew none of this, just that the e-mail said he should contact a man called Mohamed Armas and even given an address. Now, Lindey was suspicious. If this was a true lead to the people related to Jesus healed people, was he being given an opportunity to find them, or was he doing the work for another, more sinister group of people? His need to know overcame his caution, and he contacted Mohamed at the e-mail he was given. "Please, God, show me where to go to find the people whose family members you healed, let me find them, so I can understand your miraculous hand for myself."

He wanted to go on to ask about why God hadn't healed his dad, but he had been there before a thousand times. God was silent on this topic, for whatever reason, God would not give Lindey the answer he wanted. Brock, Lindey's older brother, a pastor in Atlanta, tried to comfort Lindey on their dad's "passing" as he called it. "Passing to where?" Lindey asked the day of the memorial service.

"Heaven, Lindey, you know that. Dad was close to God, he followed Jesus every day of his life, teaching at church, mentoring men, and raising us in the faith. He's not dead, Lindey, he has passed on to the dimension of life everlasting."

Lindey believed this, but his faith was on rocky soil now, turned over in the face of his loss of the one man he knew loved him unconditionally. Brock was great, a real friend as well as a brother, but he was still his brother. "Oh, Dad," Lindey cried out, "why did you have to go so soon?"

CIA Headquarters, McLean, VA

Another ominous e-mail to Dr. Batchleor, how strange. Barkley Garret saved the e-mail on the hard drive and opened up a search engine on the town of Arqa. He learned a great deal, but nothing the history books couldn't tell him. Who was this confidant, and why were they leading the professor on this wild goose chase? He watched carefully as the professor made his flight and hotel arrangements, passing them on the owner of the e-mail. His crack team finally decoded the e-mail and found the address of the sender— Arqa, Lebanon. He called the flight crew and gave them their destination. He would arrive there two days before the professor and be ready to report to his supervisors.

Boarding the plane, Philadelphia, PA

Lindey had gotten permission to take a sabbatical for three weeks to investigate the historic significance of Arqa Lebanon and how it may hold the key to finding some of the people whose descendants had experienced the healing touch of Jesus. His passport was cleared, and he was on his way to Tripoli, Lebanon within two weeks. While on the plane he continued to study the history of the little town, which was now his destination. Arqa was an ancient town, over five thousand years old based on the archaeology done in the town.

It had been an important town for many different people groups, and now it was controlled by the Sunni faith of the Muslim people. Alexander Serverus was indeed from Arqa and was one of the successful emperors of his time. He ruled for thirteen years, was assassinated and be replaced by Maximus Thrax, who was a cruel leader who had a particular hatred for the growing Christian religion. He sent Roman soldiers to every small town in the kingdom, seeking out certain families, and wiping out every relative of those families. He tried to do an ancestry search for Alexander Serverus, but could only trace him back to when his family moved to Arqa two hundred years before his birth. What was his significance here? Why did the e-mail tell him to connect with Mohamed Armas, an antiquities expert who had a solid resume, at least what was printed on the internet. Lindey laid his head back and prepared for the long trip. He slipped into a sound sleep and began to dream.

He is in the dessert, it is pitch-black, except for light coming from around the door of a small hut. He hears loud voices, they something being slammed against the wall. There are screams now in a different but familiar language. Lindey runs to the door, but can't open it. The screams grow louder and more intense, and the door shakes as someone slams against it. "I didn't tell him, I swear it!!" the voice pleads with someone for mercy. "He knew about it before we met, someone must have told him about the secret meeting place of the Healed Ones, how did he know about it?" More cursing from the assailant, and more pleading from the man against the door. "He said it was in the dessert, beyond the ruins, in a valley with three stones pointing three different directions. He said it was the stone pointing north that led to the entrance. How could he know that, how?"

There was a loud thud against the door, as a long blade slipped between the wooden slats, dripping in a red, sticky substance. Lindey knew what had happened, even as he awoke abruptly from the dream. Grabbing his phone, he opened the notes app and wrote down exactly what he remembered from the dream. What was happening? He never remembered his dreams like this or felt such emotion from them. Did this happen already? Was he part of this event? He could only ponder this and wait for the plane to touch down in Tripoli.

Akifah, known to Lindey as Sophie Johnson, waited in the baggage area as flight 2485 from Philadelphia, PA arrived and disembarked. She knew exactly what Dr. Batchleor looked like, but she needed to pretend that she was clueless to his real mission. She got herself assigned as his translator by the Lebanon visitor bureau and waited to take the fly into the spider's web. She was dressed in all white, tight fitting but not too tight. She understood Americans to be preoccupied with the flesh, something she had used against men from an early age. Most men were weak, selfish, lustful, and lonely. They were easily seduced, and easily used for the mission she was assigned to. This professor would be no different, and she would soon watch him die with the filthy SOTH at his side. She held up the sign with his name and pretended to not see him as he walked toward her.

"Hello," Lindey said as he came upon the young beautiful lady holding a sign with his name on it. "Dr. Batchleor, I presume," Akifah said in mocked surprise and delight.

"Yes, I am finally here, and I am tired, hungry, and looking forward to getting started first thing tomorrow."

Akifah smiled, "I am Sophie Johnson your translator and tour guide while you are in Lebanon, and my orders are to assist you in any way you need while you are here. Would you like to eat at an American restaurant, or try something local?"

"Local of course," Lindey said, "and call me Lindey, I'm not comfortable with the whole professor doctor titles."

Humility, eh? Akifah was impressed and a little taken aback. This man feigned simplicity, not formality. "Then Lindey it is, and you can call me Sophie. Come along, and we will get you settled in your room, then go out for some local fare."

She ushered him into a car with a driver who looked like the size of an SUV himself. He took the bags and deftly stowed them in the trunk, then opened the door and moved swiftly to the driver side. Lindey thought he noticed a large, holstered handgun underneath the pressed suit as the man settled into the car. He guessed it was because of all the unrest in the country, and actually felt safer because of it. The next twenty-five minutes exposed him to the most aggressive, life-threatening ride of his life. He sweated in spite of the air-conditioning. They stopped in front of a five star hotel, and entered. Once checked in, Lindey showered and shaved and dressed in much lighter garb to endure the heat that assaulted him whenever he left the confines of an air-conditioned space.

The local restaurant was impeccable, and Lindey was delighted by the tastes and smells he experienced that evening. "Sophie" seemed eager to hear about his experiences in America, she was like a child listening to a story that was too good to believe. She asked probing questions, but did not take any question to the personal side. She was a consummate professional, and would serve Lindey well as he embarked on this journey. The dream was still bugging him, coming to his consciousness often during the day. They agreed to get an early start, and Sophie said she had already contacted the antiques dealer and set up an appointment for 9:00 a.m. Lindey was starting to experience jet lag, and Sophie could see he was starting to fall asleep in his chair. He was asleep before his head hit the pillow and awakened with a start as the phone called him to consciousness. No dream, no foreboding, just delightful deep sleep.

The ride to the antiquity dealer was short and reckless. The driver seemed to be able to slip between stalled cars as if by magic. Lindey got out as Sophie was rounding the back of the car. They looked around at their surroundings and wondered why an established business would be right in the middle of a residential area. Mohamed met them as they pushed open the door. "Come, come, my new friends, come out of the heat and find comfort and welcome in my store."

Lindey did a 360 as he was amazed at the amount of historic material that was packed in every crevasse of the little store. Mohamed was a dealer in rare Roman artifacts, gleaning many of them from back room deals with local archeology groups needing additional funds for their digging projects. He had studied in Tripoli and gained a master's degree in Roman antiquity studies. His true motivation was to infiltrate the local culture and discover where certain families originated from, and where their descendants were now living. He was responsible for many deaths in the region, and with the help of local authorities loyal to the faith, those deaths were either explained or never came to light. Lindey only knew about his educational background, but had no idea he was stepping into the spider's trap.

"Mohamed, I'm here on a teaching sabbatical with a mission to understand the history of Arqa, specifically the history of Alexander Serverus. I'm writing a study on the emperors of Rome and how their leadership affected the culture and climate of the local tribes and towns. Alexander Severus seemed to have a successful though shortened stint as emperor, and his influence over local government seemed to encourage a freedom of religious expression for both Jews and Christian of that time. Can you give me the details of his time as emperor, and share with me your expertise as to how his rule affected the religious, financial, and political landscape while he served."

Mohamed was prepared for these questions and gave a lengthy but riveting response that filled in enough gaps to keep Professor Batchleor placated, but not enough to tell the entire truth. As far as Muhamad was concerned, emperor Serverus was a SOTH pig, a mutant who deserved to die at the assassin's hands. His influence allowed the Christian faith to run rampant across the region, even allowing for house churches to build permanent places of worship to this lone carpenter from amongst the Jews. His successor chose a slow painful death of poison for the Emperor, allowing Emperor Thrax to take over and begin the cleansing group's first true offensive against the SOTH.

Lindey interrupted his thoughts, "Can you take me to the ruins where Serverus lived? I'd like to see them for myself."

"Professor, I mean Lindey, I can take you wherever you want to go in Arqa. Let me make the arrangements, and I will contact you later today. Why don't you spend the afternoon walking through the town, and visit the marketplace in the center of the town. I will see to everything tomorrow."

Sophie volunteered to take Lindey around the town and show him how to barter at the market. Lindey enjoyed the back and forth negotiating, with vendors feigning surprise over the low offers made for their wares, then capitulating with regret and a friendly smile as they completed the transaction and took Lindey's money.

Sophie's phone vibrated as she received a text. It read, "Is he here, and are you prepared?"

"Yes," she responded. "We go to the ruins tomorrow. I will inform you when we find what we are looking for." There was no reply, but she knew they got her message. They would use Lindey to lead them to the SOTH living in the region, and then they would honor Allah with a bloodbath to end the battle here.

Garret had a good line of sight to Lindey's hotel room and could use thermal imaging to track his movements in the room, even with the curtains closed. He tried to do some background on this interpreter, Sophie Johnson, but he soon discovered that this person had not existed until three years ago. The backstops were very professional and would fool most people, but the software Garret used was powerful and penetrating.

He put her image into a facial recognition software and settled in for the long time it would take to identify who she really was. Mohamed, the antique dealer, was exactly who he said he was. He had a long history in Arqa and was a respected businessman in the area. It was no concern of Garret's as to how he procured his antiques, everybody was using everybody, nothing new to Garret. His attempt to clone Sophie's phone was stopped by a cloaking software that threatened to shut down his own software if he attempted to penetrate the security in the hardware of the phone. Why would a lowly interpreter need such a highly encrypted phone? More mysteries to unravel while he loosened his tie and settled in for the evening.

Lindey was dreaming again, he was at the same door, hearing the same screams and angry interrogations. He saw the blade slip through the space in the slats, then the groan of life leaving a person on the other side of the door. The blade was withdrawn, and he could hear the dull thud of a body falling to the floor. The door was flung wide open, showing a figure obscured by the light from within. He seemed to look through Lindey, as if he wasn't there.

Then as the man turned, Lindey gasped as Mohamed slowly turned and wiped the large blade with a towel. He saw a body lying on the floor, a slight form lying motionless as the blood poured out of him. Lindey couldn't identify the person, but felt he knew who it was. The door closed, and Lindey found himself on a long, dark path weaving amongst the sand dunes and rocks of Arqa. He was following someone, Sophie it looked like. They were hurrying to somewhere, and Sophie was sounding worried and frightened. "I told you not to come out here at night, Lindey, only bad people are out here at this hour." They rounded a corner and fell upon three men, all dressed in black, holding military flashlights, and carrying large, imposing looking firearms. They stopped dead in their tracks as the men raised their rifles and began to fire.

Lindey woke with a start, sweat streaming down his face in spite of the air conditioning. The dream had progressed, and he wrote down everything he could remember. What did this mean, why did it seem so real, and who should he tell? He decided to keep his dreams to himself for now, and see where things progressed today. It was 6:00 a.m., and Lindey knew he would not be going back to sleep.

CHAPTER 5

It was eight in the morning when the team met for a breakfast of goat cheese, eggs, hummus, and flat bread. Mohamed told them some of the history of the ruins they would be going to today, mostly how beautiful and ornate the palace was where emperor Severus lived until his untimely death. The ruins were one mile south of the current town center of Arqa, and the last half-mile was on foot. They walked along an old riverbed, long empty of anything but sand and stones. They weaved between huge dunes and scrub trees, and the path seemed to narrow. Mohamed said that the winds would change the features of the land, often erasing one path and opening another. They came to a clearing where it seemed somebody had been taking care of. The terrain was flat, with desert flowers where a small man made water area was arranged with stone seats located around the pond like structure.

The water was pumped in from the city, and this was one of the tourist haunts used to draw people to the city. Lindey was drawn to a path leading away from the group. Everybody was enjoying the spring water made available to tourists by an old, stone dispensing hole for people to cup their hands under. Lindey seemed to be drawn to a cluster of stones at the end of the path. He noticed that each stone held the image of an animal. The image was faint, and it seemed these stones had been in place for many hundreds of years. The carved image of the desert owl faced south, while the image of the desert fox faced east. A star with five points faced west, while a lamb image graced the stone that faced north. It was this image that Lindey was drawn to.

The path weaved around through stone and sand, ending in a rock wall that looked solid and foreboding. Lindey looked at it, then looked at the right hand side where a thin crack revealed an entrance. Lindey was now on autopilot, being led in a direction he had never been, but was very familiar with. The crack revealed an opening to a large, open cave. It was considerably cooler in the cave, but that did not calm Lindey. His senses were alive, heightened by the light that was coming through the top of the cave.

The light fell on a stone table, and on the table was a scroll. Lindey picked up the scroll, carefully unrolling the cloth that held barely visible Arabic lettering on it. He carefully put it in his jacket, then turned with a start as Sophie and Mohamed called from outside the cave. They were looking for Lindey, and he had forgotten they were even there when he entered the semiconscious state that had brought him here to this cave, to this scroll, to this new clue. He shook off the moment, and called back to his team, appearing as if by magic from the concealed cave. "Where have you been, Lindey, we have been searching some time for you," Mohamed snorted with frustration and anger.

Sophie calmed the man, saying "Americans, never where you think they should be!"

There was a levity to her statement, made to lighten the moment and get them back on track.

"Why did you come here, Professor, what did you find in the cave?" Mohamed was now asking with sincere care, as one looking to help with the professors journey.

"Nothing, just an interesting rock structure that looks to pre-date the Roman occupation. Possibly used as a religious site for sacrifice, but I don't know that for sure."

Lindey kept the scroll to himself for now. He would look to it's meaning when he was alone.

"We need to double back and take the path south to the ruins, and we need to hurry if we intend to be back for dinner. My wife is cooking up a local meal that will refresh us after our long day in the desert."

Garret found it a challenge to follow the band of explorers that day. There was a fairly large group of tourists visiting the ruins that day, but his dark skin and tall stature made him stand out in the crowd, something he didn't want to do. He kept to the back of the group, lagging behind so as to follow, but not be seen by Lindey at any time.

The facial recognition software had not given him anything on the girl yet, but it was only a matter of time. If this girl had ever travelled, she would have been photographed and filed away with every person who travelled in any major airport in the world. Recognition software was very sophisticated now, and most countries shared their databases with the CIA in an effort to capture terrorists coming or going in their countries.

He managed to follow Lindey when he stepped away from his group and wandered along a solitary path on his own. Garret watched as the man disappeared into a side entrance to where? From his vantage point, he could only wait and see what happened. He watched as the antique dealer and woman came searching for Lindey. He noticed that they were talking in hushed tones, but with an air of familiarity that both confused and interested the agent. Did these two know each other before today, and if so, why had they not told Professor Batchelor about it?

The visit to the ruins was a fog for Lindey. There were plenty of interesting things to see, and Mohamed was a wealth of knowledge on the site. Lindey could not stop thinking about the cave, the scroll, the dreams, and how they all fit together. It was after 4:00 p.m. when they arrived in town, tired, thirsty, and covered in the desert sand. Mohamed told them to shower and drink plenty of fluids to properly recover from their taxing day. He would be by around 6:00 p.m. to bring them to his home. Lindey showered, drank close to a gallon of water and Gatorade, and then flopped on the bed where he dreamed.

The dinner at Mohamed's was delightful. The table was laden with every Arab treat you could imagine, from fresh hummus, avocado, cheese, and lamb followed by a Turkish coffee that was sweet as sugar and strong as a hammer. They finished with a local desert, lime cake with orange and kiwi garnishments, followed by more delicious and strong coffee. Now Lindey was awake, and he feared he would not sleep for days! Everybody left feeling well fed and welcomed into the extended family that was Mohamed's.

Lindey was still wide-awake at 2:00 a.m. when he went outside to get some air. The desert cooled in the evening, and it was a brisk walk to the ruins that Lindey was looking for. Halfway down the road, he noticed a car pulling up behind him. It was Sophie. She couldn't sleep either and noticed the professor walking out of the hotel.

"Dr. Batchleor, I mean Lindey, it is not safe to be out in the evening, there are people in Arqa like any small town who like to prey on the tourists who venture out for an evening stroll."

Just like the dream, Lindey thought, almost the exact verbiage. What next, a group of men jump out and ambush them? But he remembered that happened at the mouth of the cave.

"Come with me, Sophie, I want to show you something."

Lindey led her to the path he had gone on earlier that day, but when they came to the bend in the path, he slowed down and spoke in whispers. "Do you believe in dreams, Sophie, I mean do you believe people can receive messages somehow in their dreams?"

"Yes, I do," she said, matching his whispered tone. "Why have you brought me back here?" "Follow me," Lindey said, and they made their way around a large outcropping of desert rock, taking a route that would put them parallel to the opening of the cave he was in that day.

As they rounded the small mound, they saw a light flicker on, then off, on then off, on then off. They crouched down and looked between some rocks to see a group of men standing guard, looking down the path, expecting to see someone. One of the was using a lighter to light a cigarette. That was the flicker they saw. They were dressed in black and heavily armed. "Just like the dream," Lindey gasped, almost giving away their position. Sophie just looked at him with a mixture of awe and surprise.

"You dreamed this, Lindey, you saw this moment in a dream?"

"Most of it, with some difference, but I knew we would face certain death if we continued down that path."

Yes, Dr. Batchelor, you would have faced death, a death I had prepared for you after the night of torture and truth finding, Sophie thought to herself. It was perfectly planned. Lead the professor back to the cave, find out what he discovered, and end his life in a painful and mysterious manner, where his bones would not be discovered for weeks. How did he know? How did he know?

Back at the hotel, Lindey struggled to understand what happened tonight. He was saved from certain capture, maybe even death, and because of that dream. What was happening? He gently lifted the scroll from the compartment in his suitcase and turned on the desk lamp. The cloth looked very old, and the writing was almost gone in some spots. This was a Hebrew text he was looking at, amazing! He was well versed in Hebrew but struggled with the local accents that added characters and took away some.

It was a song of sorts with two verses and a chorus that repeated three times. He could get the gist of it and came to understand it was a story of a man, God, and a family of people called the sect of the healed. The song praised God for healing and strength, and promised to keep the secret safe through all generations until the great awakening was called into being. He took a swig of water and accidently sprayed some on the cloth. The writing changed, became darker in image. Lindey carefully sprinkled a little more water on the cloth, revealing a group of characters under and between the normal characters that had not shown in the dry condition. He eventually doused the entire scroll in water and marveled at the appearance of additional words, and a map of sorts.

Lindey was able to decipher that deep in the cave was a stone that would release an opening to a subterranean space whose purpose was to protect the sect of the healed, the people touched by Jesus. Why did they need protection? Who was after them? Was that why this group of men were there last night? Lindey's head was spinning as he took many pictures to document the additional writing that was fading as the cloth began to dry. He made sure to capture the details of the map digitally, so he could use it to return the next day to the cave.

The next morning found the group eating well and downing large cups of strong coffee. Lindey indicated that he wanted to go back to the cave and explore it further. Mohamed told him that he had been told by the local tourism leader that the cave was off limits, and a guard had been placed there to make sure no other tourists risked injury going inside the cave.

Somebody had found out about his little adventure, and they did not want a repeat visit. "Look, guys, I really need to get in there. I think there is a place further back that leads to an old underground shelter of sorts."

"And how would you know that, Professor? I have never heard of such a place, and I have lived her for over forty-five years." Mohamed could barely control his emotions as he knew the rumors of such a place, a place where the SOTH slipped away to on the great day of cleansing under Emperor Thrax.

The emperor had come to the town at night, ready to expose and kill over fifty people he suspected to be part of the filthy SOTH group. Somehow, they discovered his plan and disappeared into the desert. Their tracks led the soldiers to the rocks around the base of the first Emperors estate, but they lost the trail at the base of a small cave. They scoured the cave, searching for days to find the hiding place of the SOTH. They gave up after a week, and emperor Thrax moved on to other towns in his mission to eradicate the world of the repulsive creatures he hunted.

"Here, look at this." Lindey unrolled the scroll and revealed the unique way the cloth revealed the secrets of where the site was. "I don't know who left this for me to find, or why we encountered such opposition last night, but I am compelled to find that structure and see what artifacts it holds for us to discover."

Mohamed knew that this discovery could never come to light, and that Professor Batchelor would have to die in order to keep this from the public. He looked at "Sophie" and knew she had the same idea.

Garret's room, Aqba Lebanon

Garret read the e-mail three times, trying to understand its meaning. It was from his superiors, telling him to stand down, close the operation, and return home today. What was going on? Why did he have to follow Professor Batchelor to this town, only to leave him behind in the middle of a surveillance? He notified his team and packed up the equipment. Little did he know that his superiors were signing the professor's death warrant.

Mohamed returned with bad news. The local authorities would not allow them in the cave. There was nothing they could do. Sophie moved away from the crowd and sent a text to her contacts. Within one hour, the locals capitulated, having been called by their superiors and told to let the group into the cave in the afternoon. Lindey couldn't believe it, and Mohamed smiled in delight, but also in sadness that another life would have to end in the name of the Cleansing Group's mission.

Around 3:00 p.m., Lindey, Mohamed, and Sophie entered the cave. Lindey looked in the back of the cave, where, with the help of several flashlights, found what he was looking for. The writings from pictures on his phone pieced together to show the clusters of rocks that would reveal the entrance to the site they were looking for. Lindey used a small mallet to remove some of the back wall which had been covered with many small rockslides over the centuries. He kept looking at his phone, guided by the map and a sense that he would find the next step to meeting a family member of a Jesus-healed person.

The mallet stuck something that made a dull thud, not the ringing sound the rocks had been making as he chipped them away. As he brushed away the rubble, he discovered a circular handle, with a hole in the middle. It looked to be an opening for a key of some sort, and Lindey's heart sank. How would they find a key to this lock, and where would they start looking?

SOTH headquarters, underground facility outside Naples, Italy

"He is close to finding the truth," she said as they gathered in the large subterranean room.

This room was lead lined, sound proof, and bristling with technology. Each person there knew the situation was dire as they had never met together until this time. Sarah, the leader, spoke as she sat down. "If he finds the secret place, he may piece together the rest of our plan. We must move up the timetable. Edgar, are you ready to communicate with all of the SOTH members through secure channels?" Edgar had just arrived at the secure underground facility, and wheeled his chair up to the large table everyone was seated around.

"I can contact the ones who are still on the grid, but I'm afraid many have gone offline in order to protect their families. We will have to send people out to their last known location and go from there."

By now, Edgar had compiled a list of over five hundred families that fit the unique DNA algorithm he used to identify them across the world. He had kept good records of their location, but never compiled a digital list that could be found and used to end them all.

"We must gather the artifacts now and make our statement to the world!" cried Kreeger Phillips, a SOTH member living in Scotland at the time.

His heritage was well known as his family had served in many capacities in the government and local churches. He traced his lineage back to the man who was healed at the pool of Siloam. His relative cried out to Jesus to be healed. When Jesus asked him why he hadn't dipped in the pool, as it was said an angel stirred the waters regularly, the man said he could never get to the water in time before somebody else got healed. Jesus felt compassion for this man who wanted to be healed, and he touched him right there. The man went on to become a Jesus follower. He was crushed by the carpenter's death, then elated by the stories of resurrection. He was one of the five hundred who actually saw Jesus in his resurrected body before he returned to the father. The synagogue came down hard on anybody claiming to have seen Jesus after his death. The leaders were confounded that they couldn't find the body, and they knew if they didn't, people would actually believe Jesus did raise up and go to God in power.

Kreeger retained some residual properties passed down from that healing as did every family member born from the males of the family. Kreeger became a successful doctor with innate abilities to see inside a person to get at the real issue of their illness. He had perfected a unique procedure where using just his fingers, he could understand the issue, and, through precise manipulations of tissue and bone, effect healing that modern medicine couldn't understand or accept.

He was ostracized by the medical world and moved to a small town in Scotland where he could serve the countryside and share his faith with those he felt directed to him by God. People came from all over the world—wealthy, famous, infamous, and needy. He charged exorbitant amounts to those who were wealthy and used the money to pay for the needy to come to him. He was a committed believer and longed for the day when he could reveal the artifacts and books passed down from his family that would prove to the world the reality of God with us in Jesus Christ.

"God is making it clear that now is the time, we must act!" Kreeger said with passion and angst in his voice.

"Yes, it is clear that we need to make our statement before the Cleansing Group finishes their evil task in wiping out every member of the SOTH," Sarah said.

"All the artifacts, even the Ark?" one of the others said.

"Yes," she said, "the Ark, the cup, the scrolls, the nails from the cross, everything, all in the open, all to glorify God and bring his people to Him"

"Edgar, send the message out, we will meet here in three weeks."

CHAPTER 6

Arqa, Lebanon

Dejected and confused, Lindey wandered around the town on his own, wondering why he was running into dead ends right when he felt he was on to something solid. He found himself wandering into the local museum of Arqa. It was actually nice, with air conditioning, and many tables and walls covered with Arqa history and artifacts.

He followed the timeline laid out it the room with the earliest artifacts in the beginning, making a semi circle around the large, open room. Lindey saw a pattern in the antiques with each successive conquering force laying down its own culture and control. Control, wasn't that what it was all about? Every world order was about control, wasn't it? Each new form of government promising peace and prosperity, only to degrade into chaos and a fight for control. It seemed that man was destined to move from one power grab to the next. He even saw it in the major religions of the world.

They all promised something, but demanded obedience and punished those who resisted. He appreciated the American attempt at self-rule and relative freedom for its people. That freedom had been tested in the fires of the civil war, where a God-fearing man, Abraham Lincoln, led a war-weary nation back to healing and reconciliation. But his life was snuffed out by villains who rejected unity and peace, people who wanted to control the destiny of this upstart nation, and make it in their image. Today, the country still struggled with its freedom, as the culture slipped farther and farther away from the ideal the framers of the constitution dreamed for the people they served.

The struggle for freedom and control was visceral at times, as people forgot how to argue, disagree, and still find common ground. Lindey had been raised in a non-denominational church, one that emphasized relationship over religion, following the teachings of Jesus over the traditions of religion. He learned what it meant to not just know about God, but to know him, really know him. He recalled the moments in his life when he actively pursed that relationship, and he longed for those simpler days before the world got crazy and before his dad got sick.

Lindey eventually made it to the section of history during which Alexander Severus ruled. The collection showed he was a man of many books and scrolls, as well as artwork extolling the beauty of nature instead of the half nude art of so many other rulers of the time. There was a collection of pottery and utensils of the time, knives, forks, cups, plates, bowls, and, what was that? Lindey leaned in at took a closer look. The artifact was sitting with a collection of tools and carving instruments, only it wasn't a tool, it was a key! Lindey knew for certain that this was the key they needed to get into the cave entrance. He brought up the picture of the keyhole and saw the match was perfect. This was it, but now how could he get it and make it to the cave before the authorities jailed him for stealing?

Sophie risked the chance of a phone call while Lindey was wandering the town. She spoke to an assistant who connected her to one of the leaders of the Cleansing Groups located in Egypt. This man was the keeper of the history of the group and managed their affairs in the central Arab region. Through the years, the group had diversified into many shell companies, hiding their exploits through a complicated web of disinformation and counter intelligence.

The group was a fragile, unwitting alliance of religious, political, and financial forces, each working with the other for the unifying purpose of eradicating the world of the relatives of the Jesus healed people. Some wanted the sect to end so their own religious goals would be met. Others saw the SOTH as a threat to their power base, while others hated the message the SOTH portrayed, one of love, strength, holiness, and peace. These were not their world goals, quite the opposite. They envisioned a world where the few strong would rule the many weak, and power would be held by those who controlled the financial, religious, political, and cultural pillars of the world.

"Has he found it?" the voice asked in hushed tones.

"Yes, but there is a problem. We need a key to gain entrance, and we have no idea where to look."

"Allah will direct your path, just pray and trust. Let me know what you find, then kill the American and return to your home."

"After I have wiped out the filth that destroyed my family so many years ago," Sophie said.

"No, you must not allow your anger to rule your decisions. If we wait too long, others will discover what we have been doing, and sweep in to snatch the professor away. No, he must die now, not later. Get the scrolls, and come back, that is an order."

Sophie hung up and kicked the ground in frustration. She was so close to honoring her family by killing the SOTH who wiped out her family so many centuries ago. She could not allow this moment to pass without finding out who the leaders were and killing them with her own hands.

Lindey waited until they had finished dinner and were sitting on the porch outside the rooms they were living in. "Guys, I saw the key, I know where it is!"

"What?" Sophie and Mohamed said almost in unison.

"I was in the museum, looking at the artifacts when I saw it lying amongst a group of hand tools from the Roman time period. I matched it with the picture I took, and it is the key, I'll swear to it."

Mohamed asked in hushed tones, "How do we get it, Lindey? The museum is closed, and we do not have enough pull to ask for them to give us to the key."

"We take it, tonight, after the town is asleep," Lindey responded in equally hushed but excited tones. "Steal an artifact from a renowned museum, are you mad, Dr. Batchelor?"

"Not steal," Lindey said, "only borrowing it for a few hours. We'll return it before the morning so no one will be the wiser."

Sophie added her objection to the discussion. Lindey, if we get caught, we will all go to jail for a very long time. Can't we wait and make some calls to the authorities? Somebody did us a favor already, maybe they could do it again?"

"And about that so called favor, who did make that call, and how did they know our situation"

The professor was becoming curious and asking too many questions Mohamed thought. He feared what would happen to him if he got too close to the truth with the spider assassin hanging around. "We have to move tonight before anybody finds out what we are looking for and gets to it first. Mohamed, how are you at picking locks?"

"I am no expert, my friend, and I'm afraid the security system would find us out before we set foot in the building."

"I'll give it a try," Sophie said sheepishly and somewhat nervously. "You can pick a lock?" Lindey asked. "My father taught me how to get myself out of situations men might want to place me in. Picking locks and injuring body parts were my specialty."

The men looked at each other then at Sophie with respect and some fear as the let the statement sink in. "If I don't help, you'll only try it yourself and get caught. Let's put a plan together and come back here around 2:00 a.m.

It was late at night, and the town was asleep. They discovered with delight that the small museum didn't even have an alarm system. Sophie picked the lock in two minutes. They used the outside light streaming through the many windows to guide them to the section where Lindey saw the key. Sophie slipped under the security section, lifted the front glass, and slipped the key out without disturbing anything. In five minutes, they were clear of the building and making their way to the cave.

It seemed that the town could only afford to have a guard during the day when tourists abounded. The cave entrance was free of prying eyes. Once inside the cave, they switched on their flashlights and moved quickly to the area Lindey have unearthed. Lindey took the key and slipped it into the hole. It was difficult to work the key in the lock as there was centuries of decay and dirt inside the lock mechanism. Eventually, Lindey felt the key drop deeper into the lock where he worked it both directions until it locked into place and released the gears. Dust and rock fell all around them as a small opening to a larger cave ground into view. Lindey went in first and was impressed with what he saw. He waited for them all to enter and stand up, hoping all their lights could find the end of the cave.

They could not as the place was enormous. It was a combination of natural stone and carved out sections that acted as places to sleep, tables to work on, and fire pits to be used for cooking. The ceiling was irregular, but allowed for about twenty feet of headspace for most of the way around. There were old cooking utensils, pots, tools, and scrolls, many scrolls. Most were falling apart and becoming dust, but some were still intact as they were made on high-grade papyrus preserved over time.

Mohamed was thrilled to be in the place he had heard about but could never find. Sophie was on edge as she felt herself one step closer to revenge. They carefully collected the intact scrolls and brought them to a central meeting table, perfectly round and made of stone. Light from the moon was streaming through an opening in the roof, allowing a dull amount of light to fill the room.

"What is this place?" Lindey asked once they had gathered some more scrolls to look at.

Mohamed answered, "I believe this is the sanctuary spoken about in the history of Emperor Thrax. He lost the trail of a group of militant rebels and believed they had hidden in a secret lair until he gave up the hunt."

They gathered around the scrolls and gently opened the ones that looked like they could endure the process. The scrolls were a mixture of songs, drawings, and communal journals. They told of a group of Christ followers who were hiding from the murderous Thrax.

They described themselves as the sect of the healed ones, those touched by Jesus. Lindey was thrilled at this discovery! The journals told of a group of believers who had moved to Arqa in response to the attackers from the local Jewish leaders and Roman soldiers in and around Jerusalem. They had come to Arqa seeking a peaceful place to live out their faith and raise their families.

They were led to this site over a 100 years before Thrax came, and they spent all that time enlarging and improving the cave in case they needed a place to hid from future attacks. "Why would these people need to hide from their own race? Why did the Romans help the Jewish leaders find and eradicate these people?" Lindey asked out loud, not looking for an answer, just wondering out loud about such a happening.

Mohamed mused out loud as well, "Who knows, Dr. Batchleor, perhaps they posed a threat to the organized government, maybe they were planning an uprising of some kind."

He had to be careful not to show his disgust and hatred for the SOTH, staying neutral in order to not attract attention to his real reason for being here. Sophie blurted out, "Why do you think this group of people would hide in these caves, like cowards, instead of standing up for their faith?" Sophie couldn't contain her distain for the group, and it caused a reaction from Lindey.

"Sophie, how can you come to such a conclusion? These people were not hiding out of fear, they were fighting to preserve their history and family lines."

Sophie knew she had crossed a line and backed off. "Of course, Professor, you are correct. How cruel of Emperor Thrax to hunt down and kill people whose only crime was to have experienced some sort of healing from the man from Nazareth who claimed to be the son of God."

Lindey agreed, "You're right, Sophie, it just doesn't make sense that an emperor would personally oversee a campaign of this sort. He had legions of officers who could have covered the ground and made the arrests. It almost seems like he had a personal vendetta against the SOTH as they called themselves."

Oh great, Sophie thought, now she had ramped up Lindey's interest in Thrax's cleansing campaign. They looked at more of the scrolls and made up their minds to bring back only the ones that could survive the trip back home. There, they would be looked over by experts, and a new vein in history would be opened for all to see. This was better than Lindey had hoped for, and exactly what Mohamed and Sophie did not want to hear. They would have to wait for the right moment to steal the scrolls, murder Lindey, and make it look like a robbery gone bad.

Suddenly, they heard a sound in the back of the cave. It was the sound of something falling off a shelf and landing on stone. All three flashlights moved to the sound. They came to the back of the cave, looked to the right and the left. It was then that they saw the old man. He was standing next to a pile of utensils, one of which was still falling to the floor from the shelf he had bumped into. He was old, slumped over, showing many years of living in the hot sun. They stared at each other for what seemed like minutes. "Who are you, sir, and how did you come to be in this cave?" Mohamed demanded, almost acting out of fear and disbelief that the man could show up without them knowing.

"Who I am is not important, who Professor Batchelor is looking for is why I am here."

"How do you know who I am?" Lindey asked.

"We have been aware of your presence since the day you arrived. We have watched God lead you to this place. It is God's will that you know about this place, and it is God's will that you continue on your journey to find your path back to the savior." He smiled when he finished this statement.

"I can introduce you to some of the relatives of the people who stayed here so many years ago, when hatred ruled this land, even as it does today."

"You know people who are related to this SOTH group?" Lindey gasped.

"Yes Dr. Batchleor, They are alive and serving God all these years, in spite of the hateful group that still hunts them today."

He glared at Mohamed, but Lindey did not comprehend the look. Mohamed did and knew that this old man's life would have to end before the light of day came. "Then take us to them, please," Lindey asked.

"I cannot, Dr. Batchelor, I am only a messenger sent to help you start your journey. It will be difficult, and you cannot trust anybody who is not with us." He looked at Sophie this time, but with fatherly affection not hatred in his eyes. "Look for instructions in your hotel room that will give you the next step in your journey. I would ask you to keep this place a secret, but I know that is not possible." Again a glaring look in Mohamed's direction. Lindey seemed to discern a resentful look in Mohamed's face and demeanor. What was going on between these two?

"Please return the key before the museum opens. You will need to exit the way you came if you want to make it back to the museum on time. Bless you, Dr. Batchelor, God is using you to bring about a great awakening, one that will lead many to the savior's side. Goodbye for now, may God be with you all."

All at once, their light went out. They were thrown into darkness, but some light began to shine through the opening where they had first read the scrolls. The next moment the flashlights came on, revealing only three people in the cave. For now, they would keep the cave and the scrolls a secret until they were finished their journey to find the SOTH families still living. They rushed out of the cave, stashed the scrolls in their car trunk, and made it just in time to be let into the museum by a middle aged, hard-nosed guard who never said a word. He opened the door, waited for them to return, and then entered the building locking the door behind him. They retuned to the hotel determined to take the next steps they were given to find this special group of people. Lindey wondered what he would ask them, what stories of history would they reveal? Sophie could only imagine her time of revenge when the SOTH would pay for the destruction of her family.

Back in the hotel room, Lindey opened a small envelope lying on his bed containing a mobile drive marked "begin here" on the outer shell. Lindey opened his laptop, inserted the stick, and waited for the device to boot up. Suddenly, his screen went blank, then blinked on again as if nothing had happened. Lindey opened the only file folder on the stick and saw four files. He clicked on the first file and saw an overhead shot of Arqa with the cave circled in red.

They knew he was going there, but how? There was an arrow drawn to the upper right hand section of the picture with one of the watering pools circled. That was it, nothing more. The next file contained an encrypted file he would need an expert hacker to break for him, and there were none of those around in Arqa. The last two files were blank with just a line drawn at the top of each. Lindey gathered the team in his room and shared his find with them. "This picture shows that we go to the water pool at the foot of the Severus ruins," Lindey said. "We can go as soon as we all shower, eat, and drink some large cups of that coffee." They were all interested to see what was at the pool, but for very different reasons. Sophie contacted her Egypt counter part, and was instructed to hold off killing the doctor until absolutely necessary. They would need him to complete their hunt of the SOTH leadership, and then his life could be ended anyway she would see fit.

CHAPTER 7

Lindey is standing on a small mound, looking into the blazing sun. He sees a man climbing the mound, but his back is to the sun, and Lindey can't see who it is. "Come, my son, take my yoke, for my yoke is easy, and my burden is light, and you will find rest for your soul." Lindey felt an uncommon peace accompany this voice, and he knew this was supposed to be Jesus walking up to him. "You have struggled so much with what you see as loss, and it has kept us apart far too long. I love you deeply, as I love your father deeply, more deeply than you can currently understand. You will be given the chance to share my love with the world, but be careful of those around you. I will guide, protect, and empower you, my son, just trust me, trust me, trust me." Then he saw another figure coming into view beside the first figure. "Lindey, oh my dear son, Lindey, it's okay, everything is going to be okay." Was he looking at his father?

Lindey awoke disoriented and wondering what had just happened. He had fallen asleep after his shower and must have dreamed. But was it a dream? He was still filled with a feeling of peace, love, and longing. He longed to see his father again, just to hold him and enjoy his comforting voice. But it was his voice in the dream, and he called him Lindey. "Take my yoke," the figure said. "Take my yoke, and find rest for your soul." Lindey would keep this dream to himself, and remember the warning to watch himself around every person he travelled with.

Aboard a private CIA plane, somewhere over the country of Spain

Garret adjusted the laptop so the screen was available only to him. He was on the last leg of the journey back to the states, and he was still confused and frustrated. Why had he been pulled from the mission, and what was waiting for him back at the office that was so important it would take him out of the field? His facial recognition software had still not identified the woman who acted as an interpreter and in country guide for Dr. Batchelor. How could she hide her identity in today's digital world? The antique dealer still showed himself to be exactly what he seemed to be, but the two of them were more than recent acquaintances.

They were in this together, whatever "this" was. He switched his screen to the CIA dark website, the one most employees didn't know existed. Once on the website, he could connect safely with country agents and information hubs used to assemble and disperse current intel on anything and anybody they wanted to know about. He attempted to access information about the leadership in the Arqa region. He had a hunch about the girl and her role in guiding the doctor to his destinations while in country. He collected all the names of ISIS and Al Quida operatives, and digitally circulated the picture of the girl to every agent in the area. If she had operated in their grid before, they may recognize her and help him understand who she was.

Underground facility outside of Naples, Italy

The SOTH leaders gathered in the vault, spent some time in prayer and worship, then, believing God was leading them, got down to business. "Andrew took a big chance contacting Professor Batchelor," Kreeger said as they all sat down.

"I have already downloaded the doctor's entire laptop," Edgar said as he typed away at his own laptop. Part of the file on the memory stick Lindey had downloaded contained one of Edgar's tracing bugs. "We have searched for any record he has kept regarding his interest in the SOTH. Apart from his own blog, he seems to be getting help from several people in country. They are an antiquities dealer named Mohamed, and a Sophie Johnson, an interpreter, as their passports read. I did a bio search on both. The man is a legitimate antique dealer and archeology expert living in Arqa. The girl is more of a mystery. She only shows a professional history of three years, then it goes blank. "She is one of the leaders of the cleansing group, Akifah is her true name I believe," said Sarah, the leader of the SOTH.

"How do you know this?" Edgar asked.

"It came to me last night as a warning from God. God has chosen Lindey to aid us in the great awakening. He will use his expertise in historic relics, and together, we will release the artifacts and proof that will open one last ingathering of God's people before the door is shut forever."

The group was stunned by her revelation, but they all knew this was from God, and it would happen just as she had said. "I need more time to safely inform and direct the SOTH I have identified so they can make their way to the gathering place," Edgar said. "Jennie, can you assist me with the new software I have created for our adversaries?"

"Yes, Dr. Collingsworth, I can have the first version ready to infect their computers by tomorrow."

Jennie was a SOTH family member living in France who had been introduced to the group at an early age. Her heritage was from the lineage of a little girl possessed by an evil spirit. Her mother came to Jesus and begged him to heal her daughter. Jesus replied that he had been sent to the Jewish people, and she was a Gentile. He asked her, "It isn't right to take food from the children and throw it to the dogs, is it?"

This play on words wasn't lost on the woman, as she replied, "Yes, but even the dogs are allowed to eat the scraps from the children's plate."

Jesus loved this kind of verbal sparring, but he also loved the woman and her child deeply. "Good answer! Go home, for the demon has left your daughter."

She went home and found her daughter lying still and peaceful. The demon was gone, and their new life had begun. She became a Christ follower, and her family was dispersed with the rest of the faithful when the great cleansing of 70 AD happened. Jennie knew she was special as soon as she could talk and write.

It seemed that her family had possessed the ability to stand against spiritual attacks and teach others how to use the spiritual weapons at their disposal to fight the spiritual battles God would bring them into at certain times in history. There were times when entire nations and countries stood at the crossroads of destruction and decay, only to see a generation of people rise up in faith and strength, Leading the people to a higher way of living and loving. It was never the philosophers or the earth worshippers who overcame these crucial times of turning. They always seemed to fall to the times and become part of the enemy's plans not wanting to see man rise up with moral and spiritual courage.

This group of the SOTH membership had influenced cultures by prayer and spiritual ministry and had overcome the enemy at times when only prayer and spiritual weapons would prevail. Jennie had committed her life to Jesus at age five and amazed her parents with her ability to read and understand spiritual concepts at such an early age. But it was in the world of technology where she truly excelled. By age twelve, she was building and running computer stations for the SOTH in six different European countries. By sixteen, her parents allowed her to become part of the inner core where she worked with Edgar to develop software and hardware to be used in the great awakening. It was time to go on the offensive, take out the Cleansing Group's surveillance systems, and call the body of Christ to the great awakening.

Arqa, Lebanon

Lindey stood at the pool and watched the water cascade out of the stone reservoir into other catch basins that dribbled water out, making it easier for tourists to cup hands and drink from the many outlets created by the architect of the water sculpture. He looked at the picture, followed the arrow to this pool, and looked around him. What was he looking for? Where should he look? He breathed a prayer, a child's prayer, asking God to show him where to look. A man came up behind him, tossing a large coin into the pool, where several hundred coins now rested. Lindey didn't see him as much as he felt him move into his space, then move out again. He didn't say a word, and never looked at Lindey, so I seemed like a legitimate crowd fed collision.

Two minutes later, Lindey felt a vibration in his pocket and pulled out a small, basic mobile phone. He pressed the green button and said, "Who is this, and how did you get this phone in my pocket?"

"Calm yourself, Dr. Batchelor, there is no need to be upset. We are the next leg of your journey to the SOTH. The man you are with is too dangerous to keep as a travel partner. He is part of an adversarial group that could bring great harm to you if they feel you are getting too close to finding out about them and their plans for the SOTH. You will need to send him on an errand, then quickly leave Arqa for a place we will text to you once you are safely on the road. Use only this phone, as your personal phone is bugged by at least two different entities. You must meet with Samuel Granger in Tripoli tonight before you start your journey to Italy. There are several artifacts you will need to bring with you that will prove you have been with the SOTH here. Stay close to the phone, and trust God to keep you safe."

The caller hung up before Lindey could even get one word in.

"Who was that?" Sophie asked, saddling up to Lindey wearing a fashionable outfit designed to take a man's thoughts off ruins and put them on something else.

"Oh, on this phone, oh, just a colleague in the states asking when I will be returning. Something about a lost syllabus they need for a class this week."

He was terrible at lying and hoped Sophie wouldn't see the phone was not his own. "Okay, but we need to be back to the hotel by 4:00 p.m. so Mohamed can take back to this house for another local meal."

Lindey knew they would never make that dinner, and he started to make a plan for how he would get out of town with time to leave no tracks as to his destination.

Garret's e-mail alarmed as a communication from one of his agents loaded. He opened it and began to read:

61

Commander Garret, this is Almad Jaziq in Tripoli. The woman you are interested in is an international spy and assassin. We have been hunting her for years, and she has single-hand-edly eliminated any agent that has gotten close to her. She is called the black widow, and she is extremely dangerous. Tell us where she is, and stay clear until we can assemble a strike unit to neutralize her. I await your response.

Now Garret was totally confused. What was Professor Batchelor doing with a world-renowned assassin? Why was she posing as his in country guide? He contacted his superiors, and in ten minutes, they had him turning the private jet around to return to Arqa in all haste. He would land in Tripoli, contact Almad, and lead his strike team to Arqa to deal with the black widow.

Lindey asked Sophie to meet him at the local Starbucks equiv-alent at around three that afternoon. He broke the news to her straightforward. He drove up and motioned her into the car. "I need to leave Muhamed here in Arqa, Sophie," Lindey said when they were in the car.

"Why, Professor, I mean, Lindey, why should we leave Mohamed behind at this time in our journey?"

"I can't tell you right now, but trust me when I say it will be bet-ter to take this part of the journey by ourselves." Akifah stammered out. "I will pack my things and meet you in the lobby by 3:30."

What she really meant is that she would go up to her room, call Mohamed, and usher the good doctor out of the lobby, by gun point if needed. "No need to pack, I already have our things in the trunk. We are on our way to Tripoli, then Italy, if things go well in town this evening." Sophie just stared at him in confusion and despair. She was not ready for this weak American male to act in such a strong and unexpected manner. She just faced forward and made new plans to allow the game to play out, hopeful to get her chance at revenge before she was force to end his life.

Nobody noticed the small overhead drone that ran a parallel track with the car. Staying low and out of sight, the drone matched every turn and move the car made, as its operator swiftly altered course to keep up. Out in the dessert, it would be hard to trail after a car without being seen. This handy device had infrared, radar, and night vision capabilities, more than enough speed to keep up with the automobile bouncing along the road. The old man had many tricks up his sleeve, and the small team with him assured him that they would be ready to "guide" Professor Bachelor to his next point of contact from Tripoli to the small town in Italy where he would meet the leadership of the SOTH that covered the country in its web.

Akifah, or Sophie as she was called by Lindey, was infuriated that she could not call her contact and let him know their plans. It would be suspicious if she even tried. "What do you know about Mohamed, Sophie, and why were you so reluctant to leave him in Arqa?" Now, she had to tread lightly, play the part of the innocent young interpreter, and put his mind at ease. "I know as much as you do, Lindey, he is an antiquity dealer and local historian."

"Why do you think he was so interested in finding the old man? He spent the entire day searching the region, and I think he even asked the museum to help."

How did he know that? Mohamed had told her that he had bribed the other guard to tell him the identity of the man they had met in the cave last night. The guard didn't know, but he did point Mohamed to a local elder who would know any of the older men in the town. Mohamed had gone to "lean" on the man and get the name of the old man. She had only found this out from a text sent from Mohamed as she waited at the café for Lindey to show up. This American was smarter than she had first believed, and he seemed to be getting information from a source she could not identify. She would have to stay in character and not reveal her true goal until it was too late for him.

"I'm not sure what you mean, Professor. He seems like a kind, knowledgeable, and helpful local who was committed to helping us uncover the mystery of this group of people, the SOTH I think you called them."

"That is what they called themselves," Lindey countered. "Have you ever heard of such a group around here, or even in the region for that matter."

"No," she lied, "I still don't understand what their significance is to your historical studies of the area. They seem like so many groups that popped up and vanished across the centuries of tribes and sects." There, now she was the student, and he was the teacher again. "This sect was unique because they had been with and were healed by the man who claimed to be the son of God, Jesus Christ. They claimed to possess special powers as a result of the healing power of Jesus, and they passed these unique abilities down to their families up until today. There may be family members today who still contain the unique DNA that caused the special abilities to be shared down through so many relatives. I wonder about what the old man said, to beware of a group that stood against this sect?"

"Who would want to silence such an innocent and harmless group of people?" She almost choked on those words, as she remembered the stories passed down to her family about the death of an entire town, including most of her family. They travelled the rest of the way in relative silence, with Lindey thinking through all he had experienced these past days, and Akifah planning the next actions she would take when they arrived in Tripoli.

Garret arrived back in Tripoli at five thirty that evening. He walked up to the large SUV and was met by Almad Jaziq. "Commander, thank you for coming back to help us. We sent a team to Arqa as it is only forty minutes away. They found nothing there, but the local police had just found a local antiques dealer dead from a gunshot wound to the head. They told us this man had been a companion of the other two we are looking for. They do not know who killed the man. They gave us pictures of the professor and the assassin, who is going by the name Sophie for this operation."

"What operation, Almad? The professor is here on a historical study of the region. I can guarantee you he is no spy, CIA operative, or an operative of any other country. I have surveilled him for months, and he is just who he says he is."

"Then why does the black widow pursue him, and play the part of a lowly interpreter?" Garret didn't have an answer for that question, but he did intend to find out.

"We can only assume they have come here, to Tripoli, to continue their mission," Almad said. "I wonder how we will be able to find them in a city this large."

"No problem there, Almad, just get me a clear line of site to the CIA eye in the sky, and I will show you a nice piece of American know how at work."

He meant the software system installed on Lindey's desktop, they one he used to keep tabs on everything he said and did. Once his laptop was booted up, he engaged the software and saw...nothing. What? Why was the screen blank? He should be seeing Lindey's laptop, even if it was closed. He should be able to pinpoint his position immediately, and all he had was a blank screen.

Jennie smiled as she watched her newest anti software bug destroy the code the CIA had installed on the good doctor's laptop. Now, they would have the advantage, and they would be able to control the board, at least for now. God would help them in their mission, and this American would be blessed to be part of the great revealing.

CHAPTER 8

Half way to Tripoli, the burn phone in Lindey's shirt began to vibrate. "Hello, Professor Batchelor, this is Samuel Granger. You will meet me at the address I will text to you when we hang up. This phone is set up with a detailed map software of Tripoli and a GPS system that will take you on a circuitous route to our meeting place. I will observe and let you know if you are being followed. By no means is your interpreter to make any calls or texts while you are navigating here. If she does, we will cut off communications, and you will have to return to the states without completing your mission to find us and understand what we have to offer the world. Do you understand and agree to these terms, Professor?"

Lindey glanced over to Sophie, who was looking expectantly at him. "Yes, I understand and agree to your terms. Please transmit the address and start the software."

Instantly, the phone went dark, then booted up again, displaying a detailed map with a yellow arrow. Their car was the arrow, and it was on a route to somewhere in the city. "Who was that, Lindey, and what did you just agree to?" Sophie asked.

"I agreed to be shown to our next link in the journey. He is waiting for us at the end of this navigation."

Sophie said, "I need to call my boss and let him know where I am. I was not supposed to leave Arqa without letting him know."

Lindey replied, "Don't make that call, Sophie, if you do, we will lose this opportunity to meet some of the SOTH families we are being directed to."

"But I must check in, or they will be worried about me," she lied, wanting desperately to make contact and get the back up she needed. "They will know, somehow they will know, and our journey will end here. It's your call, Sophie, you decide where we go from here."

Lindey offered a prayer to God that she would see reason and elect to keep her phone off at this time. She complied, and allowed Lindey to watch as she powered down the phone and tossed it in the open compartment between them.

It took longer than it should have to get to this address, but the software was designed to direct them in a confusing, backtracking direction in order to confirm if any car may be tailing them. When Samuel was convinced they were alone, he guided them into the small side street, and into the warehouse door that slid up enough to let them in and rolled down just as they got into the space. It was pitch black once they turned the car off, but a single light came on in front of them, obscuring their view of the person holding the light.

"Thank you, Professor, for your patience in allowing such a long and winding trail to our meeting spot. You had some pretty bad fellows hunting you in Arqa, and we didn't want them getting in the way of the next leg of your journey to the SOTH leaders." There it was, Sophie smiled, the confirmation that they would be travelling into the heart of the SOTH leadership, right where she had been hoping to go. Her mission was almost at an end, where she would dispatch them all in a manner fitting for the cowardly people they were.

Samuel continued, "Do you know a CIA agent called Garret Barkley? You should, as he has been surveilling you for quite some time."

Lindey was speechless. Who was this Garret Barkley, and why would the CIA be tracking a lowly professor of a small private college? "He installed a tracking device in your laptop that we have neutralized, and he is now searching for you in this town." Lindey still couldn't believe what he was hearing. "How do you know all this, Samuel, and how have you been able to gain access to my laptop if it's never been out of my possession?"

Then he thought about the memory stick he received in Arqa, and it all made sense. "I apologize for infecting your laptop with our own software, but it was the only way to free you from their surveillance."

Samuel led them down a set of stairs to a well-lighted, comfortable room. "Please take some nourishment and wine to strengthen you on your next leg of the journey."

He handed them plates where they ate a meal of bread, cheese, dried fish, and lamb. They washed their meal down with a local wine and took a minute to take in all that had befallen them. "Why are you helping us, Samuel, why are the SOTH leading me make contact with them?"

"You are very important to the mission, Professor, God has made it clear to our leaders. You will carry this on your way to Tartus."

He handed an ornate box, heavy with metal corners and a lead lined top. Lindey opened the box only to find three large metal nails as well as a smaller, sharper nail, maybe made of an ancient ore, as they were heavily pitted, and seemed to be covered with a red hue.

"You are holding the nails used to hold our savior on the cross as he paid the price we all should have paid," Samuel said this in hushed and reverent tones, bowing his head as he spoke.

"Wait a minute, Samuel, are you telling me I'm holding the nails of the cross of Christ?"

"Yes, Professor Batchelor, and this will be your ticket to the next stop on your journey, Tartus, Syria."

"How will we ever cross the border?" Sophie asked, clearly taken off her game, and clearly stunned by the archeological find Lindey was holding.

"I have made the necessary arrangements and created the paperwork and passports for both of you."

He walked over to an old file cabinet, pulled on a door, and produced two manila packets. In each packet was a passport, paperwork describing them as traveling archeologists from Lebanon, and orders from the Syrian government to be let across the border without incident.

"Wow," Lindey said, "You must know people in high places."

"God is the highest place I could hope for professor, and he has allowed us to find the right people to help us get you out of town and into Syria, where you will book flight to Naples, Italy. It is there you will find the SOTH leaders and help us with our mission."

Garett was stunned. Who could have neutralized his software, and how did they do it right in front of him and his team? Tripoli wasn't a huge city, but with no way to monitor the professor's every step, he had no where to start to look. He ordered agents at every place a person would use to escape the city, from airports public and private, to bus stops, taxi stands, and even the Uber system was hacked and tracked. If they made a move to leave the city, he would know.

Samuel returned dressed in a classic Bedouin outfit, making him look like all the local vendors and market people working in the city. "Come, Professor, it is time we started our journey. Tonight, we cross the border, and tomorrow, you fly to Italy. Now, follow me to the car, keep your heads down, and try not to be noticed."

They exited a back door that led them down an ally to another garage type building. Samuel opened a door, and pressed a garage door button, the door squeaked and squalled, but eventually opened to reveal an old land rover packed with their bags and additional necessities. Samuel beckoned them to enter the back seats, and they were off to Syria.

Thy were an hour into the two-hour drive to Tartus, Syria, when they came upon the lonely outpost that was the Lebanon-Syria border. "Let me do the talking here. Remember you are two archaeologists on your way to a dig. Do not respond to any questions or challenges you may hear. Remember, you are Italian and do not understand English very well. I will do all the talking needed to get us across the border."

Lindey and Sophie looked at each other, clearly uncomfortable with the subterfuge they were being thrown into. They checked their passports again to be sure they knew their new names, birthdays, addresses, and past places they had supposedly been to. They pulled up to the border and held their breath.

Samuel was good at this spy stuff they thought. He had them across the border in under ten minutes. As they pulled away, Lindey asked, "Heard a little of what you said, but how did you get us across so easily?"

Samuel smiled, "I spoke the international language of money, Professor, 1000.00 American dollars can turn a lot of heads at the border."

Lindey was amazed at the way they had escaped the CIA team back in Arqa and felt that he was being guided somehow, led to a place he knew would be dangerous, but would be part of God's will. He kept remembering the dream where his father told him it would all be okay. How he longed for his father at this time.

Suddenly, as they veered around a sharp corner, they were confronted by the high beams of three large vehicles and no way to get around them. Samuel put the truck in park and said a prayer for protection, wisdom, and favor. Once they had stopped, the lights came down, and a small man jumped down from one of the trucks, ambling over to them like a man who was on a mission.

"You are from Lebanon, yes?" He spoke in broken English.

Lindey almost spoke when he remembered to stay in character. Samuel spoke, "We are on holiday to Tartus. These people are a pair of archaeological students with permission from the government to be here. Here are our papers."

Lindey was frightened and Sophie seemed to be as well, but she kept staring at the crowd of soldiers gathered around them, almost looking like a person doing an assessment of the situation.

"We think you are spies, sent from Lebanon to find our weaknesses and exploit them when you come to invade and conquer us this summer," Samuel said nothing, but remained steadfast and innocent, even taken aback a little to be questioned by this lower level soldier of the Syrian army.

Then it happened. The officer broke off his speech, as if he had forgotten what he was going to say. He stood there for what seem like minutes, but is was only seconds. His eyes rolled up, and he dropped straight down to his knees, then fell to his side, a small spray of red oozing from a wound on his neck. Five other men went down before they knew they were being attacked, from the ground and the air. Two strong but subdued blasts happened under the trucks to either side of them. Anybody in the trucks were instantly killed, leaving only about ten men surrounding the three prisoners. Samuel had ducked and pulled Lindey and Sophie to the ground at the first sign of the attack.

He was pulling them back to the land rover, and they buckled to their knees just as the blasts went off. Samuel tore around the last truck just as it too lifted into the air and caught fire. He never looked back for five minutes, but took the Land Rover to speeds it had probably never experienced before. "What just happened?" Lindey cried out as they sped toward Tartus.

"We got caught in the crossfire between the government and rebels," Samuel explained as he navigated the curves of the road at a dangerous speed. "It happens often just near the border where there are many rebels crossing over every day to take down the Syrian government. The rebels represent a more traditional religion of Islam, while the Syrian government is liberal and westernized in the eyes of the jihadists. They are both committed to wiping each other out."

"I don't understand, these are people of the same religion, maybe with a couple of differences, but basically it is the same faith. Why do they continue to kill and terrorize each other?"

"Sunni and Shiite are similar in some ways, Professor Batchelor, but very different in just as many ways."

"Yes," Lindey said, "but that would be like Catholics in America killing Baptists because they believe differently?"

"Don't you remember the dark ages, Professor, when the Catholic Church burned at the stake those who would not pledge loyalty to the church. The church burned all the Bibles expect the ones owned by the priests. This led to the dark ages when the common man could not turn to scriptures to find his way back to God. Then there were the crusades where the church went on a rampage, killing any heathen or Muslim who would not renounce Islam and turn to the church."

"But the Muslims were just as bloody, killing thousands in their own religious campaigns," Lindey countered. "Yes, Professor, man has inked a bloody path from Calvary to today. So much madness and bloodshed done in the name of their gods, which were their religions."

Lindey thought about that last statement. It was true that many religious leaders were committed to control and financial gain, as well as tradition and power. He remembered his father's words when he was young, "Religion kills, but a relationship with God brings life. Any man can follow God and know him daily without the control and legalism that much of religion brings with it."

Sophie bit her tongue, wanting so much to jump into the conversation and dispel the ignorance she heard coming from these infidel's mouths. Didn't they know that Allah was love, logic, justice, and order? A life lived in obedience and submission leads to a life blessed by Allah. Religion to her was her savior, not some uneducated carpenter pretending to be a Jewish prophet. She could never bow to a man who was born under suspicion and who died a condemned man's death on a Roman cross.

"And what about all of the terror going on now in the name of religion? What fool would follow a faith that encourages violence, female subservience, cruelty to children, and death to those who will not convert?" Samuel spit these words out with contempt and disgust.

"I speak of those who use Islam to commit these horrible acts, not the many who are simply deceived by their religion." Now Sophie had to respond. "Enough, I will not allow you to defame my faith and question the civility of it. My life is one of commitment, loyalty, discipline, and faith, and I take my vows to Islam very seriously. Allah requires absolute faith and obedience, and I work every day to bring honor to his name."

It was quiet for several moments as the men listened to Sophie defend her faith.

"Islam is the final word from God, but we honor the men of the book who served God as well. They were great men, men of nobility and honor, good men who are revered in the Torah and the Quran," Lindey responded, and his tone was gentle and kind. "Sophie, I hear you say that Jesus was a good man, a man revered by your faith. I have a problem with that, and here it is. Jesus wasn't a nice man, a good man, or even a great man. He never claimed to be those things. He did claim to be God, the Son of God, the only one who can forgive sins, raise people from the dead, and raise himself after his own death."

"Now to make these statements, Jesus would have to be a liar, taking all of his disciples on a one way trip to nowhere, or he was a lunatic, who actually believed the bombastic things he said about himself. I would have no interest following a liar or a lunatic. But if the claims made by Jesus and the New Testament are true, then he is Lord, Lord of all and Lord over my life. Christianity is the only faith to make the claim that God came into our world to make a way to know us personally and intimately by his sacrifice for man's sins on an execution cross. His life, crucifixion, death, and resurrection demand we come to him as Lord and abandon our worldly thoughts about how good he was."

Sophie didn't know how to respond. She had never heard this argument before. She was stunned by such a simple but profound description of Jesus. Lindey changed the conversation by asking Samuel if he was part of the SOTH members hiding in the area. "I wouldn't say we are hiding, but rather protecting that which God has entrusted to us until the time for the great revealing is to come."

"What is this great revealing, Samuel?" Lindey asked.

"It will be the moment the world sees and hears the call of God. We will gather all of the artifacts, papers, historical relics, and proof of the Christian faith, and we will share it all with the world. Our desire is to be used by God to open the hearts of millions at the last ingathering. The cross nails you hold are but a small part of the evidence we will pour out when the time is come."

"What do you mean artifacts and historical relics?" Lindey asked.

"You don't mean things like the cup of Christ, or the Ark of the Covenant, do you?"

Samuel drove in silence, with a slight grin on his face.

"You *do* mean things like that, don't you?" Lindey was almost shaking with anticipation of seeing the evidence the SOTH had collected the past two thousand years. This revealing Samuel talked about would have to be well choreographed to be taken in all at once. "We have waited for technology to give us the venue to bring our message and proof to as many people at once in the world. Ten years ago, we felt directed by God to begin the preparations for the great revealing. We have been fighting so many evil factions for so many years, people who would crush the truth and replace it with their own lies and evil. Now, we are ready to bring the world God's message one more time before the end comes."

"The end?" Lindey questioned. "What? The literal end of the world?"

"Yes, Professor, the beginning of the end times, what is described in the last book of the Bible. The times are coming quickly, and we all have to play the part God has planned for us. My calling is to bring you safely to your next contact, then slip away and prepare my own family for the great revealing. Your part, Professor, I do not know, but God will show you his plans for your life, and he will protect, empower, and strengthen you for what is ahead."

Lindey was rocked to sleep by the motion of the car, and he began to dream…

Lindey is in a valley, filled with fruit trees of every kind, as well as vegetables and spices of every variety. A wide, deep river passes through the valley, bringing life to the plants and trees. This is the river of life, and Lindey is in the valley of life. Suddenly, a bright light appears on the horizon. It is too bright to look directly at, but Lindey is not afraid. Time stands still as the light approaches. The birds and animals, Lindey has just realized were around him, all turn toward the light, but not in fear, rather in awe and reverence. One by one, they bow or lay face down in the lush meadow or in the many trees that hold them. Lindey knows this is God, and he is overtaken by holiness, righteousness, and fear. He is drawn to God and knows he can endure this fiery test of his faith. He feels the heat first as a burning cold, almost like icicles penetrating every pore. Then the heat comes, and he feels like his flesh is burning off.

He wants to scream in pain, but he can't because he is floating in a crucible, floating in what seems like molten silver. He winces in pain as a large metal scoop dips into the solution, bringing out dark material that has floated to the top of the liquid. The pain is excruciating, but he knows it has to happen. Over and over, the workman scoops out the darker material, and the solution takes on a bright silver color, with not even one spot of darker material left.

The crucible he is in is lifted onto a rack where the heat dissipates quickly, and he feels his flesh returning to his body. The cool returns quickly, and he feel cleaner, lighter, but broken and humbled. He knows he has endured the cleansing fire of the Lord, and his heart burns with power and joy. This is what God meant when he spoke through the psalmist about silver, dross, and the removal of dross until the vessel contains only pure ore—pain that brings purity, heat that brings healing, all from the hand of a loving but holy God.

Lindey woke with a start and saw Sophie sitting next to him, staring at him in terror. "I saw your face shine, Lindey, shine like I was holding a light to you, but I wasn't. You looked like a man standing in the presence of God."

She was terrified and spell bound by the experience, and Lindey was just as overwhelmed by the dream, if it was a dream. "We are here, my friends," Samuel said as they came upon an exit that went down into a large parking garage that was closed for the evening.

They drove to the lowest section, parked near a heavy door, and entered. The place was Spartan, with a community sleeping area, a small refrigerator and several lamps set around a large, round table. "I apologize for the sparse surroundings, but we must stay completely invisible until we go to the airport. I do not see any adversaries tracking us at this time, but you never know. We will turn in now and rise early enough to travel to the airport to get the first flight out of town.

The next day, they arrived at the airport by 7:00 a.m. They had tickets booked under their new names, and by 8:30 a.m., they were in the air on the way to Naples, Italy. This time, it was Akifah's turn to dream.

She is on a hilltop overlooking a beautiful valley. Life is everywhere, with plants, animals, and birds of every species dancing on the wind. She is under a great tree, shaded from the sun. She sees a man climbing the hill, obviously coming to meet her. She stiffens, as she always has around a man she has not yet controlled. This man is different. He looks around thirty with Arabic features like her, hair falling around his shoulders, and dressed in a comfortable dessert outfit. "Child," he breathes out as he comes near. "Child, why do you kick against the goad? Is it not right to follow the true God, the one who has loved you at your birth, and has loved you ever since?"

Akifah could not speak. She felt enveloped in love, totally surrounded, no indwelt with love. Her heart basked in this new love, a love born of total commitment, not one based on performance and religious activity, but a love between two people who were totally smitten by each other.

She fell back on to the tree, her eyes filled with tears of joy, and her mind taking in many new thoughts coming from the man standing in front of her. This was Jesus, the man she had mocked for so long, the faith she had built arguments against. Now she just sat there, receiving the love from God, and love she had never felt before in her Islamic faith. There was no intimacy there, no grace or mercy, just obedience, submission, and hope for a new life after death in jihad here on earth. All the fight was out of her, she just cried like a little child. And now, she was in his arms, being held gently but securely. "You are so loved, my child, and so mistaken about who I am. Trust me, Akifah, I am not finished with you, and I will never forsake you."

She awoke to an announcement that the plane was landing in Naples in thirty minutes. She looked over to Lindey who was eying her with concern. "Are you okay, Sophie? You were asleep for a long time and seemed to be dreaming a lot. You were crying a little too. Here, use my handkerchief to clean up. We will be landing soon."

Sophie was still waking up, trying to understand the dream she had just experienced. Why did she feel so full, so…complete?

CHAPTER 9

Naples airport was chaos on steroids. There were too many people, and they all seemed to be confused as to where to go. It took Lindey and Sophie an hour to find their bags, get to the taxi stand, and get in for the ride to the hotel that the Samuel had reserved for them. They were given a package when they checked in and made their way to the two rooms adjacent to each other on the fourth floor. Sophie unpacked and met Lindey in his room to open the plainly wrapped package. It contained a burn phone, a map, and an address. Almost immediately, the phone chirped to life with a text. "Be careful to watch your every step. People know you are here, and they are searching to find you. We will direct you to an exit they do not know about. Be at the address below at 2:00 a.m. tonight. Bring the map and phone. Don't forget the special gift you were given as well. We look forward to greeting you both in the healer's name."

It was 4:00 p.m., so they went downstairs to eat an early dinner and prepare for the next leg of their journey.

"Are you okay, Sophie?" Lindey asked with that same face of concern. "I am well. Lindey, just a little tired from all the travel. I haven't been a very helpful interpreter for you, as most of the people we met spoke English. I don't know why I am still part of your journey, but I feel I must be here for a reason. Perhaps Allah will reveal it to me if I spend some time in prayer after our meal."

She was actually planning to call her superiors, let them know where she was, and make plans to meet with them. She was still troubled by the dream, still affected by the sense of love that had penetrated her so deeply. She had stored so much hatred and bitterness toward the SOTH, but it seemed that had been draining away from her even now. She knew she would make the right decision when the time came, but what would that decision be? No, stop thinking about it, you must complete the mission, what you have worked for the past ten years. She still had her anger toward the people who killed her family so many years ago, that would do for now.

Garret arrived in Tartus the morning Lindey and Sophie flew to Italy. He had gotten a lead from one of his agents that a person of interest had popped up on their radar in Tartus. Garret met with his agent, only to find the man had disappeared, literally disappeared from the room they were holding him in. They locked down the whole block, but found no trace of the man. He spent the afternoon looking at each flight camera, the ones that took videos of every person boarding a plane. There, there they were! Now he had them. He called his contacts in Naples and rushed to the private plane that would get them there by evening.

Lindey spoke to Sophie while they finished their meal, "Sophie, I apologize for being argumentative in the car. I know you are Muslim and may not believe the Bible or the claims Jesus made about himself. I wanted to make sure you understood that the Christian faith has many different kinds of people pursuing God, religion, power, or control. The God I serve, actually the God I am getting to know all over again, he is a loving grace filled, merciful father who welcomes any one who comes to him. My own father put it well when he said, 'Lindey, there are many ways to Jesus, but only one way to God, and that is through Jesus his son.'"

Sophie didn't bring in the typical responses to this line of argument because she didn't have any. She just listened and remembered the dream.

The address they were given as to a church nearby. San Lorenzo Maggiore. After booting up his laptop, Lindey did a search and found the church to have a rich history. It was built on the precise geographical center of the original Roman city built there so many years ago. Beneath the church was the Macellum of Naples, a Roman market that had been excavated and restored. A mudslide had covered and preserved the market, and now it was revealed for the world to see. The site had been constructed around the fourth century BC, and the church had gone through various renditions depending on which government was in charge at the time.

They took the map, which resembled a map of a storm sewer system, with tunnel-like structures heading in all directions. There was a light colored line giving directions to navigate through the system, but where was this underground passage way? Sophie dismissed herself and finally had her chance to make her call. Her superiors were enraged by her lack of contact until she told them of her travels, and that she was about to be introduced to the SOTH leadership the next day.

"Good, good Akifah, Allah has blessed your efforts, and soon will bring you into the lion's den. Stay close to the professor, and make sure you contact us when the time is right. We are so close to knowing all the places the SOTH pigs are hiding in, and soon we will end their miserable lives once and for all."

Sophie listened to their words, but they did not excite her with visions of revenge and blood. She simply could not feel the anger and hatred she had felt the day before. It was as if a toxin, no, a poison was being drained out of her, but not by her action. She was confused and anxious, but she went along with the leaders rant, and promised to check in more regularly. What was happening to her? She ended the call, spoke to Lindey one more time, and laid down for a few hours sleep before they began their nocturnal journey.

They both woke at 1:00 a.m., dressed in dark clothing, and moved down the stairs to an exit in the rear of the hotel. Immediately, the phone chirped to life with another text. "Stop, turn back, they are waiting for you there. Take the stairs to the basement and wait there."

They walked back in, took the stairs to the basement, and waited in the storage room the stairs led to. It was almost ten minutes until they heard a faint scraping on the stairs above. Someone was coming. The door to the room they were in opened slowly, and a young man whispered, "Professor Batchelor, are you down here?"

"Yes," Lindey answered, "we are over here."

"Good, good, I'm glad you got my text."

"How can you know where we are at with such accuracy?" Sophie asked, a little taken back at the enhanced technology this group possessed.

"We like to keep our guests safe, and this town is not safe at night. Please, follow me. We will take a different way to the church."

He took them down some hallways and into a narrow hall that sloped downwards. At the end of the hall, they stood at an old wooden door. It looked ancient, but with a modern lock that had been added. They young man produced a key, and unlocked the door.

The room the entered look like a museum from the past. Old wooden boxes lined one wall, while a wall full of shelves filled with musty books and antiques filled the other. The man walked straight to the back of the room and moved aside a large box. There was a small door, about four feet high by three feet wide that also looked old but sturdy. The man produced another key, and they entered the tunnel.

Garret pulled up to the hotel, looking anxious but resolute. His superiors had ordered him to take both Lindey and the girl into protective custody, and bring them back to the states for questioning. He sent his agents around to every possible exit and then entered the front door. He showed the desk clerk his credentials and asked for the rooms they were staying in. Three agents went with him, keeping a wary eye out for anything out of the ordinary.

Garret stood in front of the door, slid the key card into the slot, and entered the room slow and low. Within seconds, he knew his quarry was not there. He called to his team to see if they had caught them trying to escape, but nobody had seen them. Once again, they had slipped through his grasp. They could not be doing this on their own, they had to be getting help. Who was giving it to them, and why?

Somewhere in the tunnels under Naples

Justin, the name the young man gave them, navigated the tunnels like he had lived there all his life. Lindey noticed the distinct Roman cobblestone lining the path beneath them. The arched ceiling also spoke of Roman architecture. "Where are we, Justin, and how can we be travelling on a Roman built tunnel system?"

"This used to be the old city of Gomad, a Roman center of trade that was covered over, sealed and forgotten in the past. It is only known to a few families, and my family is tasked with keeping it maintained and passable for any who need a quick and secure exit from the center of city to other less patrolled places of interest. I am one of the SOTH, my family has maintained this tunnel system of over 500 years."

He went on to explain that his family descended from a Jewish fisherman who knew Peter and James, the apostles of Jesus Christ. This man was good friends with Peter and James and was amazed at the change in their lives since they met the carpenter turned prophet. Jarius, the man's name, would follow them often to listen to Jesus's words of peace, love, and hope. He and his household became followers of the way and followed Jesus until the day he was crucified. One day, when Jesus was passing through town, Jarius brought his second son, James, to Peter and asked if Jesus would heal him of his sickness. The boy would fall asleep and then go into spasms and tantrums, often screaming in pain and dementia.

Peter welcomed the man, and prayed for the boy to be healed. When nothing happened, James came and prayed, even laying his hands on the boy. The boy only screamed and moaned more vigorously, spitting and growling at the disciples. Just about then, Jesus showed up from an extended time in the wilderness, which was something he did almost every day.

"What's the problem, Peter?" Jesus asked.

"Master, we have been praying for this boy, and he seems to just be getting worse. We have prayed before and seen healing, but this is something we can't help."

"Oh, Peter, James, all of you, your faithlessness breaks my heart. Bring the boy here."

Peter went outside and brought the boy and the father in. Immediately, the boy began to growl and spit, but Jesus simply gave a stern look and said, "Come out of him and never return."

They boy screamed and fell limp in his father's arms. Jesus came over, touched his head, and the boy drew in a deep breath, opened his eyes, and cried, "Father, father, it's gone, it's gone!"

Later, when they were alone, the disciples asked about the healing. Jesus said in somber tones, "This kind of evil only comes out after much prayer and fasting"

Like all other members of the SOTH, young James acquired some talents, event miraculous power, that lingered the rest of his life. He could understand and speak other languages and would share Jesus's message with Jews from all over the world who came to Jerusalem. On a special day of Passover, while fellowshipping with his father's fishing friends, Peter and James, he experienced a powerful presence along with about 120 others in the room. With Peter leading, they all began to shout out the message of Jesus Christ, first in one language, then another.

For weeks afterward, Jarius would come up to a group of people, look into their eyes, and begin sharing the gospel in their home language. In fact, he would be able to enter any town around, strike up a conversation with a local, and within minutes be speaking to them as if he was raised in the town. Many Jews in Jerusalem became believers and joined Jarius and the Apostles of Jesus in their new found faith.

His children also possessed his abilities with languages, but in different manifestations. His family grew into a devout group of people who were committed to gathering and protecting all of the artifacts collected by the followers of Jesus. Since he was close to Peter and James, but not known to the Jewish leaders who fought to squelch this movement, he was entrusted with all the things that Jesus would be remembered by—the cup of the last supper, his clothing, his family things. At the time, these were seen as simple things worth nothing, but Jarius knew they would be important one day. Like many families of the healed, his family was hunted down and almost eradicated in the great cleansing of 70 AD, but three of his sons escaped and moved to other cities, hiding and protecting the artifacts as God had directed them.

Justin glowed with pride as he recited this history, and concluded by saying, "Today, they are all gone, only myself, my father, and my two brothers are alive to pass on the responsibility of the mission our family was given so many years ago. We have retreated down here many times when we felt threatened, or when it was obvious we were being hunted. Soon, we will come out in the light, come out to share what we have, and proclaim the reality of Jesus Christ, God amongst and with us!"

They stopped at an intersection, where one path looked much older than the other. "This is where we use your map, Professor." Justin held out his hand for the map. Lindey took the map out and handed it to Justin. They took the old path, with cobblestones worn down by thousands of travelers for the past. "This place has been kept open by my relatives for about 1500 years. Thousands have sought refuge here, from different groups, all with the same mission, to destroy and erase the truth."

"What truth do you speak about?" Sophie asked, this time with genuine interest.

"The truth about God, Jesus, and man of course," Justin responded. "History reports about a man named Jesus who, for three years, led a band of uneducated men and women, and was finally put to death for his religious blasphemy. The Bible, which is seen as a historic book by most of the world, reports his life, his love, his sacrifice, and his resurrection. They never found the body. Every other major religion has a place where their leader lies in ashes. Only Christianity speaks of a savior that rose from the grave and lives in heaven with the Father. To believe less is to not believe the Bible at all. To believe it at all means your life is changed forever."

Sophie did not argue, she took it all in, listening and learning about this new kind of faith, not a religious, do oriented faith, but a loving relationship with a God who walked with his creation, sacrificed himself for that creation, and rose in power to forever keep and love that creation. Something was happening to her, and she shuddered with awe and some fear as they travelled on. Lindey asked Justin if they were heading to the church using these tunnels.

"No, Professor, your map was split off from the original and held by another SOTH member so that there could never be a complete map of this place until the great ingathering was to come. The place under the church is a special place, but we are going on past that place to a more recently built complex designed for housing and protecting only the highest leaders of the SOTH. They have been meeting there this past week, praying, planning, and waiting for you both, Professor."

Lindey and Sophie stopped in their tracks and together turned and looked at Justin. "Yes, Sophie, you too. God has chosen you to be his protector and guide, and you have done well to get him here."

Sophie, Akifah, was flabbergasted. Did they know her true family roots? Did they know she was an assassin, ready to kill the SOTH leadership, did they know?

"What do you mean, Justin, Sophie was chosen? I met her as an assigned interpreter and guide when I landed, we've never met before."

"That is true, Professor, but I believe God chose her to help you on your journey."

So they didn't know, good. She couldn't let them suspect her true motive for sticking with the professor all this time. But now she felt different, and the burning heat of hatred and revenge was being drained away by these loving, strong yet meek Jesus believers. What was happening?

Garret knew he was close, but he couldn't figure out how they had escaped. He ordered a six-block sweep of the area, stopping every car and taxi, and checking every parking lot and garage. He booted up his laptop again and tried to engage the tracking software, but still got the blank screen just like before. He assigned some agents to the airport in case they attempted to flee, but he felt that somehow, they weren't running as much as they were being led somewhere, but where?

After another hour of maneuvering the winding passages, they arrived at a set of very old flat stone stairs leading down to an even older looking door. "I didn't think this went any further down. Justin," Lindey said.

"This was added during world war two and has been up fitted and improved ever since," answered Justin. "Please, give me your phones. They won't function here, and we don't want nosey people to find us, at least not at this time."

They handed over their phones, and followed Justin down.

The old wooden door opened to a short corridor that ended in a much newer and heavier door. It looked like a blast door from the old nuclear war bomb shelter days of the fifties. It contained a very sophisticated lock system that could only be operated from inside the facility. Justin pushed what looked like an old style doorbell. Lindey looked up where he saw Sophie looking. There in the upper right corner was a small black box with a red light blinking. They were being watched. Within moments, the door opened with a ponderous thumping, revealing that it was made of three-foot thick steel, solid steel.

They entered a large, rounded room, humming with every kind of military grade technology a small country could use to survive. There were several doors off the main facility, and they were led to one of those doors. They were in another, slightly smaller room, also curved, almost egg shaped. There was a large round conference table, with high backed seating for fifteen. They were asked to wait here for further instructions. Lindey was impressed, and Sophie was almost shaking with the conflict going on inside of her. This was the place she had dreamed about for so long. This was the opportunity she had prayed for and now she was feeling conflict, not anticipation. What would she do when the opportunity came?

"Edgar, are you certain your information is correct?" Sarah, the SOTH leader asked, sitting down at the conference table in yet another meeting room in the SOTH underground complex.

"Yes, Sarah, I am certain. The backstop software we used with Garret Barkley's laptop allowed us to look into every part of his life. He is the grandson of a SOTH operative I located fifteen years ago in America while I was using the DNA history company as a front for my work. His name is Garret Barkley Senior. Garret is related through his son, Arthur Barkley. They had one son, Garret. This is the same man we are looking at today. There is no question, he is a SOTH relative."

"Do you think he knows?" She asked.

"No, I am certain he does not. He is acting on the orders of someone in the US government, and we don't know who that is yet."

They all sat for a moment, taking in the ramifications of the information they had just received. If this CIA agent was a SOTH relative, then God must be using him for some purpose they did not understand. Sarah said, "Release his laptop, Edgar, let us see where God takes him on his journey to us."

A small, old woman entered the room where Lindey and Sophie were seated. She was bent over and walked with a cane. She was dressed in a habit worn by catholic nuns. She walked quietly to the table and sat down without making eye contact with either of them. She closed her eyes, and for five minutes stayed in that position. They were convinced she had fallen asleep. They were about to attempt to wake her when she spoke.

"God is merciful, full of grace, love, and holiness. None can approach him and live, only through the son do we see him. His plans are beyond us, and we live to serve, love, and be loved by Him." She halted and took a deep breath. "I have been sent to assess your hearts, to know if you are truly chosen by God for this task. Do you have the nails?"

Lindey produced the box with the nails from his backpack. The old woman opened the box and gently took out the three nails they had been told held Jesus to the cross some two thousand years ago. She kissed one of the nails, held them close to her heart for a minute, and then placed them back in the box. "The nails meant to end his life merely helped transition him to become the savior of the world. Glory to God and his plan to save his creation."

Lindey spoke gently, asking, "What do you mean, assess us?"

"I am a SOTH relative, my heredity goes back to a man Jesus healed of leprosy."

She then told the story from Matthew chapter eight where a man came to Jesus and asked to be healed if Jesus wanted to heal him. Jesus responded, "Of course I want to heal you, come here."

As the man approached him, flakes of skin started falling off him. By the time he fell down at Jesus's feet, he was completely healed. Jesus instructed him to go to the temple and make the appropriate sacrifices for a person healed of leprosy. This way the healing would be confirmed, and many people believed because of him. His descendants also experienced the changes in their bodies, passing down unique talent for understanding and interpreting people and their inner motivations.

Many of this family came to lead towns, build churches, and become successful doctors and political leaders. The great cleansing had taken many of this family, but down through the ages, there was always a remnant kept, they believe, by God, to continue the work of the SOTH until the healer returned for his beloved creation. "I am Ava, and God has blessed me with insight, to determine a person's true nature and spiritual condition. My gift allows me to understand the heart of a person, and their soul, to some extent. Please come near."

Lindey moved closer, and Ava took his hands. He felt a slight tingle, like an electric current running through him, and then it was gone. Ava held his hands firmly and whispered to herself for a moment. "You are an honest man, Professor, you came to know God at an early age. You struggle with pain and sorrow from loss of those you love. You question if God is good, if he really cares, if you really matter to him. You have studied history to understand man's search for God, and you hope to find him again for yourself. You have great faith, even if it has laid dormant these last three years. Open your heart again, Lindey, let God walk with you, learn again what it means to walk in his love. Your father waits in love for you."

Ava released his hands, and sat back in her chair. Lindey was astonished by her look into his soul. She saw the essence of who he was and where he had been. He walked to the end of the table looking a little spent and lost in his thoughts.

"Now it is your turn my child." Ava was motioning to Akifah, Sophie, to come and sit with her. Sophie knew she could not make contact or her true intentions would be revealed. "Come child, come, I must make contact for you before you see the leaders."

CHAPTER 10

CIA headquarters, Washington DC

Garret looked surprised as his laptop jumped to life and began to run its boot up system. In a couple of minutes, he was looking through his files, anxious to find if anything had been taken or altered. He found nothing except a new e-mail from a source he did not recognize. Somehow. the e-mail had circumvented the spam software designed to block out only the e-mails he wished to connect with. It simply read:

If you are truly looking for truth, find file x345klop447, and see who you really are. Be careful, you may not like what you find.

That was it. He did a hard drive search and found the file. He opened it, and it contained an address, several pictures, and a DNA code report from one of those ancestry companies.

The pictures were of some old people, one of African-American background, and the other from decidedly Arabic heritage. His eyes widened as he read the names of the people, Hannah Johnson and Garret Barkley. Who was this person? Why did he have the same name as Garret? He did a search of the address and discovered a small house in Alabama. He opened the DNA file, and read the sequencing sheet. He was not an expert on DNA sequencing, but somebody had highlighted certain parts of the code, which he interpreted as significant, but he didn't know why. He was ready to send a team to Alabama, but then he remembered the warning and kept everything to himself for now.

Something seemed familiar about the black man in the photo, but he couldn't place it. Just then, his phone buzzed and he took the call. His superiors were concerned that he had lost the two persons of interest, and they were looking for an update on where he was with the search. He danced around their questions, and promised to present them personally to the group in two days. Now he had backed himself into a corner, one he better find a way out of. The CIA had no mercy for those who could not complete a mission with total success.

Just as Sophie was planning an escape, the door was opened, and Sarah, Edgar, and the rest of the SOTH leadership entered. Ava left the room, and Sophie retreated to the back of the room near Lindey, drawing a breath of relief for not having the encounter with Ava. "Hello, Professor Batchleor, may we call you Lindey? We are the SOTH leadership, and we welcome you in the name of the healing savior Jesus Christ."

Lindey moved forward to receive their welcome. "And you, Sophie, thank you for guiding and protecting Lindey as he travelled to us. I pray that you are learning about the love the father has for you as well."

Sarah seemed to be able to see into Akifah's soul, and she knew her secret had been found out. But why were they not moving in, restraining her, and killing her for her attempt at their lives? "I believe God has been speaking to you, drawing you into his perfect love. It is love that overcomes our bitterness and misplaced loyalties, it is love that drains away the anger and revenge that drives us away from his presence."

There it was. They knew about the dreams, the thoughts she had been having even the calls she had made in the past two days. This was extraordinary, miraculous, truly something other worldly. Sarah continued, "God's purpose for you both is to understand the love of God, and trust him in the dark moments of life as well as in the celebration moments. You are each here with different agendas, and the old agendas are fading even now. Akifah, my dear child, there is no more need to hide from us, we know who you are and why you are here"

"Akifah, who is Akifah?" Lindey asked looking at the other SOTH members in the room.

Sophie spoke, "I am Akifah Lindey, that is my real name. I have no idea how they could have discovered me, but they have. I am so sorry for lying to you, Lindey. I thought I could use you to get close to them and make them pay for the death of my family so many generations ago. You see, my family tells the story about when the SOTH came to their town, moved in and took over the place of worship. They ordered my family's faith out, and took over with no love or godly care. When my family fought back and tried to take their place of worship back, the SOTH brought down a curse of disease on them, and the entire town died, except for the SOTH families. I have been waiting for the chance to exact revenge on whomever I could, waiting all these years to gain access to their lair, and kill them all for what their relatives did."

Lindey was white faced with shock, horror, and the feeling of being betrayed.

"I trusted you Sophie, Akifah, whatever your name is. I trusted you, let you in, took you into my confidence. How could you do this?"

"Be at peace, Professor," Sarah said as she laid a hand on Lindey's shoulder. "This child who was lost in her pain and bitterness is being healed even now, and it was your purpose to bring her to us to complete her healing. Akifah, the truth of the massacre at the town of Mohit is this. Yes, our people did settle in the town, and began to live, serve, and work in the town your family lived in. It was a Muslim town at that time, and the religious wars had taken their toll on many families on both sides. Those wars were not God's will but man's. Both sides believed they were achieving God's purposes by attempting to create a single religious and political power that would control and subdue the other. God was not in the murder, the rapes, the tortures, and the destruction of entire towns. Mohit was tired of losing so many to the wars. When the SOTH arrived, they lived a different kind of faith. They claimed the name of Jesus Christ, but without the trappings of any one religious order. The served the people no matter what their faith or lack of faith was. They cared for the sick and dying, even if it meant risking their own health to do so. This created a peace in the town that was truly special. The SOTH used their special gifts to bless the town, and their was genuine serenity there for several years. Then the warriors came."

"They came with their hatred, their lust, and their demands. The town resisted them, even their Muslim brothers begged them to leave them in peace. This request fell on deaf ears, as the warriors prepared to attack and slaughter the Christians in the town. Then, one evening, the Christians were praying to God for protection, strength, and guidance. They felt God tell them to warn the Muslims and other townspeople to flee the village because God was going to destroy the warriors and their camp, which was situated in the center of the town. The SOTH leader went to the Muslim leader and told him what would happen. The man went to the leaders of the Muslim people, and they met to decide what to do. Some had been swayed by the warriors, and suspected the SOTH were trying to scare them out of their homes."

"Others were close to the Christians and had been blessed by their selfless service to them when they were sick or destitute. They were split in their decisions, as one group packed up and moved off into the desert with the SOTH families. Some of your family left with them Akifah, while others stayed behind. When the Lord struck the town, anyone left there was destroyed. Two days later, the people returned to find the bodies of hundreds, fallen where they stood with a strange coloring of their skin, and a feted smell coming off the bodies. They all cried and mourned the loss, Christians with Muslims, burying the bodies, and cleaning up the town together in quiet sadness and joined sorrow. The story of the Mohit massacre spread and was colored to favor the warrior's side by stating that they were killed by the SOTH."

"It was true that God had destroyed them, but it was to protect his people, and those who were not yet his people, but may have become so in the future. Many Muslims accepted Jesus as their savior, even though it meant giving up their Muslim faith and losing their place in the Muslim community. This led to a breakdown in the precious harmony that had been there before the warriors came. It seemed that a dark cloud had entered the town and turned people against each other. Many warriors who had heard and believed the massacre lie were massing to come into the town and kill every Christian and converted Muslim that was left in the city. The SOTH sensed a terrible violence coming, and slipped out in the night, never to return to their friends again. It was then that the story was fabricated about what had happened that night. You see, Akifah, some of your family survived, and have served God with us all these years."

Akifah began to get dizzy and started to fall as Lindey caught her and led her to one of the chairs around the table. Her life the past fifteen years was a lie, fed to her by her handlers, fueling her anger and bitterness, driving her to become the killing machine they needed to do their work all over the world. She felt used, lied to, as if everything she believed, including her faith, was a lie.

Sarah seemed to sense what she was thinking. In a moment, she was kneeling in front of Akifah, and she said, "Our beliefs may cause us to stand apart, but that is never God's will. He wills for everyone who desires to know Him to come and be known. Many people have started out Muslim, Hindu, Buddhist, or non-religious. As they honestly study and learn the truths of God's word, they come to the conclusion that Jesus was who he said he was, is who he said he is today, and has the power to forgive and restore them as children of God. If they choose not accept God's offer, the are no less loved by Him or His people. The secret the townspeople shared in Mohit was this truth, the never ending love of God."

Akifah managed to speak softly, "I know what you say is true, and I have felt that unconditional love from Lindey and others, but I have not returned it as I should. My faith teaches that submission, obedience, and logic are to be worshipped above all else. We see God as a God of justice and judgment with no chance of ever getting close to or knowing him in the way you all seem to know God. I want that relationship with God, not an empty religion, I want a relationship!"

"Then you shall have one, Akifah, right here, right now. And I think you would want to start that walk with one of your relatives. Come, Dominique, meet your cousin, Akifah."

Akifah looked up in repentant tears to see a young man, tall, slight build, and with the biggest grin he could make, exposing bright teeth while tears streamed down his face. They all bent to their knees around Akifah, and Sarah led her in a prayer that was repentant, personal, and one that would forever change her life in ways she could never imagine.

As the group finished hugging and encouraging Akifah, most exited the room, while Sarah, Edgar, Keener, and several of the top leadership of the SOTH stayed behind. They all looked around the table, drying their eyes, and smiling back at Akifah as she embraced each of them, making her way around the table to Lindey. "Can you ever forgive me for lying to you, Lindey? I was a blind, bitter fool who could only see the hot coals of hatred. All of that had been extinguished in the loving presence of my Jesus, yes, my Jesus. I will understand if you no longer want me around."

Lindey lifted her chin to see her eye to eye. "Akifah, today you have become my sister in the Lord, a forever friend of Jesus and this group. Of course I forgive and restore you to my friendship and family of believers."

He embraced her for a long time, which led to more sleeves being used to wipe more tears of joy away.

Sarah spoke, "Now if we can gather ourselves, Edgar has some exciting and ominous news."

Edgar stood up and moved to the front of the room. From out of nowhere, a screen came down from the ceiling, and a projector lowered out of the ceiling. Edgar looked positively excited with the news he was going to share. "Lindey, Akifah, we apologize, but we have known about you Akifah from the day you connected with Lindey at the airport. We also knew that you were being tracked by a CIA operative named Garret Barkley. What we didn't know until yesterday was that Garret is one of us, I mean his family is a SOTH family."

The screen blinked to life, and a series of pictures of artifacts were displayed, with the words, "The SOTH initiative" typed in the header.

"The SOTH knew that a time would come when God would show the world proof of his time on earth, and the greatest act of love on the cross. Lindey brought the nails of the cross to us today, and these other artifacts have been arriving this past month at an accelerating rate."

Lindey and Akifah blinked twice to make sure they were seeing correctly. Pictures of the cup of Christ, the plate that held the bread, his headdress, single stitch clothing, as well as many of what looked like old scrolls, paintings, and all sorts of archeological finds that would be astonishing to the world if ever revealed. Then there was the Ark of the Covenant. *The* ark? Really? But where had it been? Sarah smiled as she watched them take it all in. "Yes, Professor, it is all real, and will all be revealed to the world very soon. All those Templar Knight stories you watched on cable TV, well they are mostly true. Many lost their lives hiding and protecting these precious relics against all sorts of evil. We have many adversaries who want to prevent this great revealing for diverse and equally ominous reasons. We have religious, non-religious, satanic, anarchist, and just plain governmental entities who will stop at nothing to bring us to a deadly end before we can make our statement to the world. You are both now part of this journey, and God will show us your part to play when the time comes. Go on, Edgar, tell your plans to unite the SOTH at this time."

Edgar moved on to the next slide, which showed several Ancestry DNA company logos. "For many years, I have been searching, compiling, and contacting people who carried a unique DNA sequence to their genes. Most people would not notice this sequence as anything out of the norm unless they had been instructed to find it."

The next slide was of a DNA strand. Certain sections were highlighted and enlarged.

"It was these specific strands that led me to understand the SOTH legacy. You see, I compared my gene sequence to the ones I found from my search of the DNA banks found in all of the commercial companies out there. I created an algorithm that could search for all similar DNA strands, then match them to the person who gave the sample. In the beginning, I would travel to the person's home, introduce myself, and share what I had found. I didn't realize how deep the Cleansing Group was connected. Many families died in the wake of my foolish need to meet other people like me. Then, when they killed my wife and paralyzed me, I decided to commit my life to finding and protecting the SOTH wherever I found them."

"I developed a software so sophisticated I could enter the cyberspace of any government facility in the world and never be discovered. I was able to wipe out all reference to SOTH families who suspected they had been discovered. I found new places for them to live in safety and secrecy. Many of them shared their family history with me, and some shared the artifacts passed down secretly from their families' families. Sarah and a few others with the financial means and political leverage formed this group of leaders and built this facility in secret as a means for organizing the day of the great revealing."

"I've heard that mentioned by others, what is the great revealing?" Lindey asked.

Edgar answered, "This will be the time when we will share all of these artifacts and proofs with the world in one powerful moment using the Internet and technology we have developed. Every person with a phone or computer, every company and business will see the revealing all at once."

Lindey reacted, "Sounds impossible, how can you make people see something if they aren't looking on the Internet for it?"

Sarah responded, "Text technology has advanced to the point where we can send a message to every available phone, tablet, laptop, or computer using encrypted software designed by the military and enhanced by our own computer master, Edgar."

Edgar looked around the room, brimming with pride and excitement. "Everything is in place, and the final relics are arriving this week. Our main concern is over which entity knows about this place, and if they are on their way yet. We have to assume we have been compromised at this time. Akifah, your involvement has helped us keep up with your handlers and track them through cyberspace to where they live. We have placed powerful software into their system to hide our location from them. We have even been feeding them phony updates from your phone so they do not yet suspect you have left them for your savior. Lindey, we have also been in contact with Garret, giving him the necessary information he needs to find his past, and make a decision as to what he will do with that new information. He will be in danger as soon as this is discovered, and we are praying for his safety as he journeys to us. We may be in need of his services before the time comes for the great revealing."

It was early in the morning before they ended, and they were directed to sleeping quarters on the next floor. How large was this complex, and how had they kept it hidden all these years? Lindey was exhausted and fell asleep as soon as he relaxed on the bed. He began to dream.

He is in a large room, vast and circular in shape. He's not sure because he cannot see the ceiling or the end of the room where the curved walls should come together. He senses something moving on the floor off to his right. It comes into view, and it is a large, python-like snake. It writhes toward him, a look of hunger in its eyes. Then, suddenly, it becomes a lion, prowling, looking for a meal. When it sees him, it stops dead still. The lion begins to circle Lindey, getting close with every lap. Lindey is frozen in fear but remembers his faith. He prays, "I know what you are, and in the name of my savior, Jesus, I rebuke you from this place."

The lion stumbles back as if it has been shot, but then begins to circle again. "In Jesus's name, by the power of the father, in the presence of the holy spirit, be gone!" Lindey is filled with a sense of power and loathing that is holy and angry at the same time. He shouts, "Go!" and watches as the lion twitches, writhes, becomes the snake again, and dissolves into the air around him. He then sees the meadow again, so much beauty so much peace.

His father is there, and he runs to him. They embrace, and his father cries with joy at his sons renewed heart. "I miss you so much, Lindey, but I know you are okay, as is mom and your brother and sister."

"Can you see us, Dad, do you know what is going on here on earth?"

"Yes, Lindey, it is amazing. The father allows us to participate in his redemption story, and we are praying for you and cheering you on all the time. I had no idea heaven was such an active and exciting place!"

Lindey spoke through his tears of joy. "Can I stay, Dad, just a little?"

"No son, your time is coming, but not for many years. We will never be apart, and you can count on my prayers and cheering to continue until we meet here again. Be careful of the enemy, and remember what you learned tonight about how to defeat him. He is under God's control, and has no power over you that you don't give him. Keep your friends close, and trust them when the time comes. I love you my son, now wake up, wake up!"

CHAPTER 11

The next morning, they assembled in the kitchen area to eat a meal of dried fish, cheese, bread and coffee. Lindey had a glow to his face, and Akifah smiled. "I see Jesus on your face!"

Lindey smiled, "Yes, Akifah, it was a sweet and comforting dream, filled with power, love, and my father!"

"I too had a vision, Lindey, one where I was fighting an adversary that changed from a snake to a lion to a man and then back into a snake. Every time I tried to strike it, it would back away and stalk me. I felt instructed in my soul, I know that sounds crazy, but it was a dream, I felt instructed to say the words, 'In the name of Jesus Christ, you are defeated.' I spoke those words, and the thing twitched, reduced in size, and disappeared. What do you think of that Lindey?!"

CIA Headquarters, McLean, VA

Garrett just stared at the computer screen. He had given some saliva to the CIA lab at Langley and asked for a DNA sequencing report. He did not tell them it was his, they assumed it was from one of his targets. Now, he was looking at side-by-side comparisons, his swab with the swab report placed on his laptop. They were exactly the same, or at least so close that his untrained eye could not tell a difference. He compared the highlighted areas as well, and the were perfect matches. What did this mean, who lived in Alabama, and whose DNA matched his almost perfectly?

Tehran, Iran

Omar had waited long enough. Akifah had refused to contact him once she had landed in Naples. His people there had been able to track her until the evening she disappeared, which was two days ago. It was as if she had vanished from the hotel complex. He had received several texts from her phone, but without the accepted code words, he knew this was a lie from her captors. Now Omar would find her, complete the mission, and return triumphant over the SOTH for the final time. He knew they were scheduling some sort of expose on their corrupt faith, one that would further confuse and divide the true faith of Islam.

His faith was already suffering under those who would divide and destroy the holy faith of his family, proud Shiites all of them. He never thought about why Islam had fought against itself for so many years, Sunni killing Shiite, back and forth for generations on end. He prayed to Allah for the day when the twelfth imam would return and bring religious unity to the whole world. The Mahdi, as he is called, will bring peace, justice, and unity in the name of Allah.

Omar had obeyed Allah's directions as he discerned it from the Quran, prayer, and the occasional vision or dream. Islam revered religious dreamers, those who Allah spoke directly to in their inner man. Omar had risen to a position of leadership amongst his people in Iran and in the leadership of the Cleansing Group. "We must locate her brothers, she has been amongst the blasphemers too long for safety. Perhaps there is another way to find her."

SOTH underground facility near Naples, Italy

"It will work, I'm positive," Edgar pleaded his case. "If we can create a fake meeting place, we can invite both groups, and let them fight it out."

The two groups he was referring to were the Cleansing Group and the US government people tracking them.

"But how do we convince them we are serious?" Sarah asked.

"I will contact them," Akifah said as she stood facing the group.

"Not a good idea," Edgar responded. "By now, they will think you are dead or have been compromised. They will not trust a meeting with you at this time."

"Then let's give them two targets," Lindey said. "Let me contact this Garret Barkley fellow, and invite him to meet me. Then Akifah can take a picture of me in cuffs and looking spent in a jailed room. She can convince them I have given her important information on the SOTH, but she has to bring me to them at a safe place in Naples, Italy. They will both come, I know it."

Sarah stood and walked to the front of the room. "That is a bold and risky plan, Lindey, but we have no choice. Our time draws near for the great revealing, and we need to neutralize these adversaries before our people will feel safe enough to bring their treasures to us for the event. We will provide the necessary technology for you to make contact and draw both parties in. Edgar, please make preparations for our guests to arrive."

Warrior, Alabama

Garret pulled up to the home with the Alabama address. He had taken the private jet to a small airport just twenty minutes away. Now, he sat in the rental car, wondering why he was here. He saw the door open, and an elderly woman come out. She was radiant in her complexion, and looked like a warrior queen on display. She walked to the mailbox, opened the door and glanced over her shoulder toward Garret. He slumped down in the seat and willed her to go back into the house. She did, only her husband was now walking out to the car Garret was in.

He was the man in the photograph, and then it hit him. Grandpa Barkley! This was the man his father spoke about only twice in his life. Once when he asked about his extended family when he was young, and once when he asked in his teens about where he came from, and what his family history was. His father had told him that his grandfather was a bad man, a mean man, a man who beat his wife, and tormented him until he left in his teens never to return. Garret had believed him, and never attempted to learn more. Now the man was at the car, asking Garret to roll down his window. "Can I help you, son, are you looking for somebody?"

"Yes sir, I am. I'm looking for a Garret Barkley."

"Well, here I am, sir, can I help you with something?"

Then he stepped back, looking startled and amazed. "It's you, my grandson, you're Garret Barkley, aren't you!"

Garret knew he had to come clean. "Yes, sir, my name is Garret Barkley, just like you. Some kind of coincidence, huh?"

"Well, get out of that car, and let me get a look at you."

Garret opened the door, and was immediately wrapped in a bear hug that took his breath away. "Oh, son, we have prayed for this day, prayed everyday since we heard of your birth. Welcome, son, welcome to the family!"

It was sometime in between cake and coffee that Garret got to ask some of the questions he was hoping to ask. "Grandpa, what ever happened to you, and why did my dad keep us apart?"

Garret senior looked down and heaved a big sigh. "Son, your father was a man of few words, and his attitude toward us soured as he grew older. He rejected our faith, then rejected us. He ordered us to never contact you, and to never tell you the truth about your family or he would be forced to take you away forever. We agreed, but we never gave up hope that God would lead you back to us."

Garret asked, "What truth do you need to tell me, Grandpa?"

"You have a rich family history, Garret, one that dates back to the time of Christ. Your relative, his name was Chander, Chander was forced to carry the cross beam of Christ when he could no longer carry it himself. Chander looked into the eyes of Christ as he picked up the cross. Jesus touched him, and he felt a power course through him that he had never felt before. He straightened up and carried the beam in front of Christ all the way to the hill where he was crucified. He stayed there, watching this stranger die, and curious as to why he would be killed in a way meant for thieves and murderers. He witnessed the moment Jesus died, felt the wind and heard the thunder, and yes something else. That touch had transferred something to him, something he would cherish and protect with his life and all of his family that would come after him. He joined the Christ follower movement and learned to trust Jesus as his personal savior. He baptized his entire family and lived in fellowship until the time came for him to return to Ethiopia."

"He took his family back and began to teach the way of Christ to his village. He had developed the ability to speak and read beyond the norm of that day, even self teaching the language of the Jews, so he could read and teach their books to the people. He combined this with his months of being amongst the disciples, and birthed the Christian church that would sweep across the country for centuries to come. Like many of the people affected by Jesus, he had to go into hiding when a group came claiming to know the real Jesus, and that he had been buried and dead, still in the tomb where he was placed."

"They had come to disperse this blasphemous faith and kill any who would not recant their faith. Many Ethiopians died in that clash, but Chander was secreted out of the town, and he ran for his life. He lived in obscurity with his small family, but watched with joy as the church grew and spread in his beloved country. You are a descendant of that family, Garret, the last in the line of my family. Your father knew all this, but rejected his faith and turned to worship the world and the power it promised him through the government forces he served with his life. When he disappeared, we were heart broken. We honored his request to not contact you, but we never stopped praying for God to bring us together when the time was right. Now you are here, and we are so happy!"

Garret was dumbfounded and overcome with shock angst at these revelations. He was actually a descendant of the man that carried Jesus' cross! How could this be kept from him all these years? Why did his father lie about his family, and keep his grandfather from him? He knew his father was not a religious man, that was why he too did not have an active faith. He knew there was something bigger than him, something that transcended time and space, but he didn't believe this was something that could be connected with and worshipped.

Religion was for those who needed simple answers to life's unpredictability, and he was taught that logic, reason, and knowledge would lead to a greater understanding of life better than any of the limited world religions. Now, he was sitting in a home with a family he had just met, and he was being told that he was a relative of a person who he wanted to learn a lot more about. "Grandpa, wow, I really like saying that. Grandpa, can you tell me how many of us are left that are descended from Chander?"

"It's hard to say, son, I only know that I am a descendant from the slave arm of the family. My great grandfather, Cyrus, was brought here from Ethiopia to work a farm in South Carolina. He had several children and all of them were genius level people who helped run the farm, invent ways to make farming better, and even brought running water and medical practices nobody understood. It was like they were absorbing information from another source, taking in learning that had no visible reference point of origin. The plantation owner was a man of faith, and treated the slaves like family, sharing God's love and converting many to the Christian faith. When the civil war began, the plantation was burned and the family scattered."

"Cyrus and his family travelled the underground railroad to the north, where he took up residence with a wealthy family committed to the freedom and development of the black race that had been so unfairly treated in the south. Cyrus grew in stature amongst the town folk, becoming the leading authority on black and white relationships. He used his unique talents for oratory and study to convince the town elders to allow two black men on the leadership board, and they agreed. This town was blessed with economic, social, and religious growth, becoming the envy of towns all around that were recovering from the devastation of the civil war. Cyrus was your great-great grandfather, and I am the last of our clan. You will now carry the torch for us, and we pray you will honor God with this task"

"Grandpa, I am not a man of faith, and you now know that with my CIA background, I can't just drop everything and go on a self discovery journey."

Garret Sr. smiled, "I didn't mean for you to do that, son, I know you have been away from the faith of your fathers. I only ask that you pray to God, and ask him to show you who he is. You have been given the gift of your descendant, Chander, and it will be used by God for his purposes."

SOTH underground facility near Naples, Italy

Edgar gave Akifah her phone and took her to a secure place to make the call. Omar picked up on the fourth ring. "Omar? Omar this is Akifah. I am sorry for only sending texts, and those without the proper code words."

"Input code words now or you will be disconnected."

Akifah spoke several words, and they were sufficient. "Akifah, where have you been? We tracked you to Naples, then lost you at the hotel. Did you know a CIA team has been shadowing the American since he has been here?"

"No," Akifah lied, "That is very unfortunate. I am holed up in an abandoned unit outside of town. I was able to subdue the professor, bring him out here, and begin the interrogation. He has given me some very important information I need to get in your hands, but you will have to come here to see it."

Omar was suspicious.

"Why should I come there when you can send me the information digitally?"

"Akifah said, "There are some artifacts you need to see, and they tie in with his information."

Omar thought about the risks, and then capitulated. "I will come, but only if you meet me in Naples, and we go there together."

She countered, "How will I do that if I have the professor with me?"

"Tie him up, or knock him out, I don't care, just make sure he is there when you return."

Now she had to decide, and she did. "Yes, I will meet you at the old church called San Lorenzo Maggiore."

"Good," he said, "send me the address, and I can be there is five hours."

"No, not until two days from now. I need that time to gather the things I was able to get out of him, and it will take until then. Two days, 3:00 p.m. local time. I will see you then."

"Agreed," Omar said, and the line went dead.

Now it was Lindey's turn. "I'm not very good at this, in fact I'm lousy. What if he asks me questions I can't answer?"

"Don't worry, Lindey," Akifah said, "God will give you the words to speak when they are needed."

Lindey turned on his laptop and went to the e-mail software. He sent an e-mail to himself and wrote, "Agent Garret, if you are reading this e-mail, then you know that I know who you are and what you are doing. I have information for you that will expose a dangerous group called The Cleansing Group. They are a collection of murderers, spies, and mercenaries committed to the destruction of a group of people called the 'Sect of the Healed.' They are poised to take out the leadership of these innocent people in the next few days. If you want to see them stopped, you will need to fly back to Naples, and go to the church called San Lorenzo Maggiore. The Cleansing Group will be there expecting to meet one of their spies, but they will really be meeting you. Two days, 3:00 p.m. local time. Come with a team, Mr. Barkley, it may get messy."

There, the e-mail was sent. Now they would have to wait, pray, and see where the next move would lead them.

Warrior, Alabama

Garret felt the vibration of his phone letting him know he had received an intercept e-mail. He excused himself from his grandparents and read the e-mail. He was stunned. How did Professor Batchelor know he would be intercepting his e-mails? What was this cleansing group, and how was he involved with the SOTH group? Knowing he was now a part of that group changed everything. He called the plane, and told them to book a flight plan for Naples, Italy, immediately.

He also ordered a five member assault team to meet him at the Naples airport the next day. He had two days to plan the meeting, two days to understand his new heritage and legacy, and two days to decide what his next move would be. He asked his grandparents to tell him more about the SOTH and what their goals were for the future. He listened with fascination, and began to understand where he might be fitting into this outlandish mission they had planned for the world.

On the way back to the plane, Garret checked in with his superiors and told them only what he wanted them to hear, just enough to get permission to go back to Naples the next day. It seemed that his superiors knew a lot about the SOTH, and they also sounded familiar with the Cleansing Group. They gave him the green light to travel to Naples and intercept the Cleansing Group at the church. He was instructed to take them alive, and be ready to chase down the SOTH leaders as well.

Garret knew he would not do that, but he agreed to make his priority for the sake of his superiors. They said something that stuck with him all the way to Naples. "Do not believe anything you hear about the Cleansing Group. They are actually operating within their boundaries as we set them. Do not interfere with their pursuit of the SOTH leadership. We have been using them to get to this group for some time. Professor Batchelor has been an important part of our success in tracking them to this point. We hope you can collect them at Naples, and find out what they plan to do. They are a subversive group, Garret, dangerous and unpredictable. Be very careful and trust nobody."

As he hung up the phone, the operative turned to agent Barkley, and said, "He is going to Naples, and will do as we say, sir."

Good, Garret's father thought. *Soon, I will have my quarry, and my son will be the key to my success.*

He did not know that his son had been to Alabama, had met his grandparents, and was making plans to upset everything he had planned.

CHAPTER 12

Naples, Italy

San Lorenzo Maggiore was a beautiful church with two chapels designed in the Baroque manner and a beautiful main building. Three floors now held a museum that chronicled the history of the city and the area surrounding the church. This was also a safe place for the SOTH, beginning in the thirteenth century when the church was built. One of the stone masons, Mario, was digging the foundation when he discovered the large underground chamber that would become the SOTH hiding place for hundreds of years. He was able to conceal the entrance by using foundation stone to mask where the entrance was.

He would go into the cavern after work to dig it out and enlarge the space. One day, while working on a far wall, he broke through into a tunnel like structure. He discovered an old Roman sewer system that had been buried and forgotten hundreds of years ago. He explored and opened up the passages, and passed the secret on to the other SOTH families living in Naples at the time. Soon, Justin's family would make the commitment to always keep the tunnels open for the SOTH to use.

Edgar, Lindey, Akifah, and a team of SOTH field operatives made their way to the Church cavern. It was a little more that two hours until the appointed time to meet the Cleansing group at the church. Akifah would travel to the underground entrance to the hotel Omar was waiting at, while Lindey and Edgar would proceed to the church cavern to await Garret Barkley's arrival. Lindey squeezed Akifah's arm gently as they came to the intersection. "Be careful, Akifah, I'm sure your boss will be suspicious and wary of any changes you suggest to the meeting place and time."

"Be at peace, Lindey, I know this man, his weaknesses, and his tendencies. God will show me the right way to put him at ease and draw him in."

Omar paced the floor of his penthouse room at the hotel. This was the same hotel Lindey and Akifah had escaped from just a week ago. Omar had fifteen operatives stationed around and in the hotel. He would know when Akifah was coming and would take her captive when he got the chance. How could she compromise herself this way? She was too professional to make these kinds of mistakes. Obviously she was being controlled somehow by the SOTH pigs. Omar had known Akifah since her father died in a raid in Turkey. She was only thirteen at the time, but she channeled her anger against the group Omar convinced her had killed her father and her extended family as well. The SOTH became her lifetime enemy, and her one goal in life was to locate and terminate as many of the mutant creatures as she could. Omar fed her anger and honed her into the assassin she was today. He was anxious to learn what she had gotten out of the American and how close they might be to eliminating the SOTH leadership.

Akifah popped out of the lower chamber into the basement of the hotel. She slipped into the main basement and saw that the staircase was being guarded by one of the Cleansing Group field operatives. She knew this man, and that he was not the level of fighter she was. She flung open the door and walked straight up to the man. He looked stunned to see her, and started to say something when Akifah struck him sharply in the throat. He collapsed, gasping for air. She sprayed him with a mist that Edgar had given her. It put him to sleep immediately.

Edgar said the effects were harmless, but the man would stay asleep for at least two hours. She slipped up the staircase, and into the lobby. She saw three more operatives waiting in the lobby. She didn't want to make a disturbance, and the desk clerk had left the front desk, so she slipped around the corner and squatted at the bank of key holders. She knew Omar would pick the highest room, so she took the extra key to the penthouse, and made her way around to the back stairs. Another operative had to be subdued, but she did it without making a sound. She was so good at her craft, but her heart wasn't in the hunt anymore. She had a new mission that pushed her, and she had to succeed with this ruse so the SOTH would be free to move toward the day of the great revealing.

The hallway to the Penthouse was empty, but she knew there would be cameras mounted that would capture anybody entering the hall to access the penthouse doors. She opted for a direct approach, and ran full speed for the door of the penthouse. As she reached the door, it opened just in time for her to sprint into the entrance, and turn to face one of the operatives. It was Omar, "Why do you come to me with such aggression, Akifah, you took out some men who are friends of yours."

They should be better trained to protect you, Omar, she said as she turned and walked to the bank of windows looking out over Naples. "We were very worried about you, child, you have been in the presence of the infidels for too long."

Akifah began, "They are nothing but corrupt beasts, religious idiots who think they can change the world with their silly claims."

This was a good start, she could read Omar's body language, and she could see him start to relax. "Did you get what you needed from the professor? Did you have to kill him?"

"Not yet," she lied, "he apparently knows where the SOTH leaders are gathering for their big moment, and he was almost ready to talk when you called. I have left him with one of my team to be softened up sufficiently for you to talk with directly."

"Good," Omar smiled, "he will give us what we need, and then we will cut him into pieces and spread him across the city sewer system. Why do we need to meet in this church you mentioned? What is there for us to see?"

"The church was a safe house for the SOTH in the early years. There are relics that date back to the 1400s, and some of them hold instructions as to where to find the underground tunnels the SOTH cowards have used all these years." She was being careful to give just so much away in order to draw Omar to the church, but time was running out. "We must be at the church in one hour in order to catch the SOTH leader who works there. She is a nun, and actually thinks she is safe working in a church. We will make her show us what we need, then we will send to her precious savior."

Akifah hated saying these things, but she knew she had to keep playing the part of the enraged killing machine Omar knew her to be.

"Good, Akifah, it sounds like a good plan. Let me gather the team together, and we will leave immediately."

Lindey, Edgar, and the assault team were in place waiting for their signal. Lindey asked, "Why did the church turn on the SOTH families? I thought they of all people would embrace the people healed by Jesus," Edgar sighed. "The families of the healed were mostly Jews in the beginning, but when Jesus began going to gentile towns like Decapolis, he healed hundreds of them as well. The Jewish healed ones struggled with the synagogue leaders, and many were cast out. The Gentiles didn't have any structure like that, so they began to meet together and form their own support system. After Jesus died, rose, and ordained the apostles to begin their work of redemption, many Gentile families were welcomed into the newly formed churches."

"Soon after the fall of Jerusalem in 70 AD, SOTH families spread out with the other believers, forming new churches and growing by great numbers. You know the history of the Christian faith, you are a studied professor. What you don't know is that the Catholic Church had committed to squash any movement that wasn't under their control. The Templar Knights were one such group, many of them being SOTH members as well. The church learned of the SOTH families from the torture of some of those brave Templar Knights. They sent out squads to round up and deport these families from Italy and other countries where their form of religion ruled. Many SOTH hid down here for weeks while the church went house to house looking for the SOTH. Religion is threatened when free men stand up to live in freedom and serve God in their own fashion."

"The Catholic Church probably felt they needed to protect their faith from the undisciplined and chaotic ways of the unchurched.

Order, obedience, and justice gave them absolute power amongst the ignorant illiterate people they ruled. When they couldn't convert a sinner, they tortured and killed them in most unchristian ways. I have never understood why this was accepted behavior, but the church wielded power, and they liked it."

Lindey replied, "I too have read the history of the catholic and protestant faiths, and have been amazed and disappointed at the fighting and killing that went on in the name of God. Forced conversions, soldiers raping and pillaging, it was the darkest days of our Christian faith, a time when we needed a leader to take us out of this hate filled culture."

"The SOTH sought to use their powers for uniting and healing the church, they were never a threat and never sought to overthrow the religion of their times. They wanted to live in peace with men of all faiths, and gently share their faith and their family stories with those seeking God. Their powers handed down from the first Christ healed family members were used to serve, not rule. So many families have been wiped out, or scattered across the world, hiding in secret, but always serving and loving their savior. Now, we will unite them, share their truths with the world, and overcome evil with the good news of the healing savior."

Lindey felt the phone vibrate twice in his pocket, the signal he was waiting for. "They are on their way," he said to Edgar.

"Where is Mr. Barkley?" Edgar asked. One of the field team typed in a few codes and told Edgar the CIA team was five minutes out.

"Perfect," Edgar smiled. "Garret will get here fifteen minutes before Akifah and her entourage. Lindey, go up into the church and wait at the choir loft to the left of the speakers dock. Be sure you have access to the door so you can make your exit when the time comes."

Garret was making his way through the slow, narrow roads of Naples, finalizing plans for the meeting with Professor Batchleor. He was still absorbing all that he had learned the past two days, and he knew what he would have to do when the time came. He pulled up on the east side of the church, beneath an entrance not used by the public. His team led the way, entering the large church one floor below the appointed meeting place. His team was given orders to stay out of sight until given the okay to engage the Arab terrorists that were on the way there. He was taking a big chance, as his superiors thought he was going to collect the SOTH leadership today, when in fact he was going to provide a way out for them to complete their plan for the great revealing.

Omar stopped the van, pulled over into a small parking lot, and put the van in park. "Akifah, I must know, what did they tell you about the time your family was killed, did they tell you lies about the day they killed so many of our family and friends?"

"No, Omar, they told me nothing about that time. They tried to convert me to their faith, but they did not threaten or abuse me as I expected they would. Once I refused their arguments, they stopped their evangelism of me. They left us alone for a time, and I was able to convince Professor Batchelor to follow me to a safe house where we could better evaluate what the leaders were saying to us. Now he is there, suffering under my hand, and crying like a child."

She almost choked on those words, but knew she was being tested, not completely trusted, and she had to allude suspicion until they were at the church. "I believe you my apprentice, and I trust you for now. Lead us to the church so we may progress to our goal."

Akifah directed the van to a side street where an overhead walkway to the church was connected two stories above them. She instructed them, "We will park here, enter this side building, and cross over to the church up there."

Omar ordered his troops to unload the van and make their way into the building. Omar noticed Akifah placing something in her ears as they entered the building, then he heard a faint sound that first tickled, then attacked his ears with searing pain. The last thing he saw was one of his team falling next to him.

Akifah moved to a small unit near the stairs, switched off the power, and signaled with her phone. From downstairs, a team of people dressed in similar garb as Omar's team arose and quickly transported the unconscious men downstairs, where they were transported via the tunnel system to a place they would be held until the time came to release them. Akifah felt sadness for the way she had misused Omar's trust, but this plan had to work in order to protect the SOTH until the great revealing.

Lindey felt the phone vibrate again, and he knew the next step of the plan had been accomplished. He waited for Garret to arrive and prayed for God's protection for all involved.

Garret went up one flight and entered the church. Somehow, somebody was able to close the church to visitors today, so the large meeting place was abandoned. His team fanned out and moved up toward the front of the church. He saw Professor Batchelor in the choir loft left of the speaker podium. He knew what would happen next, so he reminded his team that there would be no shooting in the church unless they were fired upon. He would secure the professor and bring him down to the back of the church.

They were to keep their positions hidden in the pews and amongst the pillars. Garret moved down the center isle, waving to the professor as he walked. Suddenly, two side doors busted open, and a team of darkly dressed men entered quickly. In seconds they were between Garret and his team. Garret seemed to be confused and hesitated for a moment. One of the invading team shot a small dart like object at Garret, and he dropped heavily to the floor. One of Garret's team did not recognize this as a sleep dart and returned what he thought to be hostile fire. Limited gunfire was exchanged, and two of the SOTH team were injured. Gas canisters were released, and soon, Garret's team was chocking and gasping as the other team dragged Garret away.

The plan had worked almost perfectly except for the dangerous gunfight that almost cost lives. Lindey had ducked for cover as soon as the first shots rang out. He was glad to see his team intact, and Garret along with them. They all hurried down the secret entrance to the tunnels and moved away from the church toward the safe building.

"Professor Batchelor, you took quite a risk up there, somebody could have gotten killed on both sides!"

"Yes, Garret, it was a risk, and please call me Lindey. Now the US government thinks you were captured by the SOTH, giving you an alibi when this is all over."

Akifah came up beside them, smiling and thanking God for their safety. "Wait a minute." Garret cried. "Aren't you the assassin so many countries are looking for, the black widow I believe?"

"That was my old name Mr. Barkley, the one I used before I met my savior. I am now just Akifah, humble servant of the healer, with much to make up for should He allow me to."

The journey back took about three hours, as they had to go slower while attending to the two wounded men. They reached the entrance and were let in by the gatekeeper. Once inside, they tended to the wounded and assessed their progress.

Sarah brought the group to attention. "We have been blessed by God to get this far, and it is obvious we will have to move quickly to bring everything together by next week. All of the needed artifacts are in place, and the computer software is ready to engage every technology available across the world. We must maintain our secrecy and safety until next week."

Garret and Lindey were relaxing in the kitchen area, sipping strong coffee and getting to know each other. "Professor, I apologize for invading your privacy and surveilling you for the government. I had no right to do that, and I am truly sorry."

Lindey smiled, "It's okay, Garret, you were following orders, and thought you were on the right team. I'm sorry that you had to find out about it in the way you did."

Garret sighed, "My father wasn't the easiest person to get along with. When my mother died, I was thirteen years old. I had no faith, so I didn't really know what happened to her. Dad said she was on the other side, and we would see her in time. I didn't know what that meant, so I always hoped I could understand some day. I pursued several religions, testing the veracity and credibility of each one. My father was okay with it until I came to the Christian faith. He did not want me pursuing that faith of lies as he called it. We never really talked about it, but I felt he had experienced something bad with his family that had led him away from that particular faith. One time, when I pressed him, he revealed that he had been raised in the church by an abusive hateful man, one who served on the church board and lived a double life at the same time. He left that hell hole as he called it when he was seventeen."

"He joined the CIA, and I soon followed as soon as I graduated from college. Dad was lost to us five years later. They never found his body, but his team assured me he had lost his life in that dessert place. I wanted to connect with what was left of my family, but I could never bring myself to meet the man who was so terrible to my dad all those years. Meeting them this week was such a blessing, but finding out about my heritage is still sinking in. My relative actually carried the cross for Jesus on his day of crucifixion. I am related to the one man Jesus blessed on the day of his death. I feel like I've been reborn into a new life. I can never go back to the CIA, I know that, and I know that I need to help you any way I can. Tell me what I can do, Lindey, how can I help the SOTH with their mission?"

Lindey looked wide eyed at Garret. "Your relative was the Ethiopian that carried the cross for Christ? That must be something to digest. I never thought my search for the relatives of the healed people would lead to this experience, but I feel that we are being led by a power from God that both directs and protects us as we listen and respond to his guidance."

"But how do I get that knowledge. Lindey, I mean, how do I discover God's plan for me?"

Lindey smiled, "I have learned to read, listen, pray, learn, obey, repeat. I read God's word, take moments to be still and listen to my inner voice, respond in prayer to God daily, humble myself to learn from others, and continue to do this daily. I will be shown through insight, physical happenings, the confirmations from other people, and peace that passes my normal idea of peace. God does not hide his will from us, but we hide ourselves from him when we live life on our terms, with our demands, our agendas, and our expectations. I am still learning that, Garret, but as imperfect as my attempts to know and follow God are, he returns my efforts with grace, mercy, love, and direction. It's not a perfect, smooth road, but it is his road, and that's the road I want to be on."

Garret chewed on those words for several minutes, while Lindey drank his coffee and gave him space. Finally, he asked Lindey, "So what is the process for knowing God, I mean Jesus, I mean, how do I put a stake in the ground and tell God I'm serious about knowing and following him?"

Once again, a small group of friends knelt together, prayed together, and welcomed a new brother into the family of God.

CHAPTER 13

Holding cell, SOTH underground Facility

Edgar approached the group of men who they had captured that evening. He found Omar and addressed him. "I am sorry for the attack on you and your team, but it couldn't be helped. You were getting too close, and we needed to replace you for our plan to work. Now, we will return you to your hotel where you will return to your country and never come back to Naples."

Omar spit at him, "You pig mutant, I will personally gut you and watch you die a slow death when I break out of here. You really think we are going to just walk away with our tails tucked between our legs? No, we will return, find this place, and wipe your filth out in one attack!"

Edgar hesitated to do what he had to do. Messing with the human mind was dangerous, but it had to be done. One by one, each team member was led to a cell where they "visited" with Edgar for ten minutes before leaving for another holding cell. Finally, Omar was led to the cell. He was tied to a chair in the center of the room. Edgar was sitting at a table a few feet away. He looked up and caught Omar's eyes. Omar blinked, try to look away, but he could not. Those fiery blue eyes, they stared right through him. He began to forget, little by little, he forgot. Suddenly, he awoke in his penthouse room at the hotel. Why was he there? Why had he come? Who was he to meet here? He could not remember. His team was equally in the dark and believed they were there to do something, but they could not remember what. Omar felt the overwhelming need to leave and go back to his headquarters, immediately. In five hours, he was in the air, headed back. What had happened these past two days? Why could he not remember?

Edgar was exhausted. He had not attempted this level of mental alteration with so many people, and he paid the price with a killer headache and nausea the entire evening. The breach had been filled temporarily, but it would not last long. Soon, Omar would be looking to make all his threats come to fruition for every member of the team.

Garret met with Sarah, Keener, Edgar, and the rest of the SOTH leadership. They had a week to prepare for the great revealing. Edgar had the list of the remaining SOTH families who possessed artifacts to share with the world. They had to meet and take possession of the relics in a way that would keep each person safe from the Cleansing Group hunting them. Garret would help them by figuring out who was manipulating the CIA and how much they knew about the SOTH. He still had access to the mainframe through a backdoor he had created two years ago when he thought of leaving the CIA. He wanted to always be able to defend himself from the long arm of the government. Now he was in, and he installed the seeker software Edgar had developed. It would back trace any e-mail coming to him and identify the place of origin. It could also snoop on the author of the e-mail, reading everything that came to their e-mail file. This would allow the SOTH to keep the CIA and their operatives at bay until the great revealing next week.

San Lorenzo Maggiore Church

Sister Anna came to the father the next morning. She was upset about what had happened at the church. There was a mess to clean up, and everybody involved had escaped before the police arrived. The police searched the church top to bottom and found nothing they could investigate. The small group of nuns responsible for caring for the church were cleaning up the mess, replacing pews that had been shot up, and wiping down the old stones stained with blood. "What happened here, Father, who were these awful men?"

Father Andre answered, "We do not know, Sister Anna, but the police are on the case and looking for the men that did this."

What Sister Anna didn't know was that father Andre was a SOTH operative, not even known to the Naples group. His family had survived the cleansing of AD 275, and they had felt led by God to use their special gifts in the organized church that would become the Catholic Church. Through the hundreds of years, many of his relatives served in small parishes, shunning the larger, more influential positions in the church. They realized those places of service would call for certain actions they were never going to take, so they stayed in the small towns, serving and sharing the true faith their families had passed down since their healing experience with the savior. Father Andre's family came from a man healed of palsy in one of the many Gentile towns visited by Jesus. He not only was healed completely, he could heal others as well. His name was Peter, and he was a humble carpenter, proud to be in the same profession as the healing savior.

Peter cried when he heard Jesus had been crucified, and he rejoiced when he heard of the resurrection. Soon, some of the apostles came to his town, and he was baptized into the family of the believers of the WAY. This was all they knew to call their newfound faith, until someone coined the word, "Christians," meaning people who believed and followed the teachings of Jesus Christ.

Peter kept his gift quiet, as he had seen the masses following Jesus just to get healed. He would use his gift only in the company of the local elders, and under their watchful eyes many were healed and restored to physical and mental health. Peter's family passed down this healing gift, always one man in each generation, never more. Andre had experienced his gift the first time when a ten-year-old friend fell out of a tree and broke his arm. Andre felt compassion and ran to the child before anybody else could get there. He prayed for the boy and watched as the bone slipped back in place and the arm was restored with no apparent damage. Only the boy who was healed fully understood what happened. When he told his father, Andre's father was told to keep his son away from the rest of the children.

The family moved away to Naples, Italy, where they began a new life as the keepers of the grounds of a beautiful church called San Lorenzo Maggiore. There was a school there, a catholic school where Andre learned much about his faith and how this religion worked. He was suspicious of the teaching that honored men and women almost as much, and sometimes more than the savior himself. He graduated and went into the priesthood, looking for an outlet for his growing faith. Andre never argued about the religious part of his faith, he just kept talking about Jesus and the word of God.

He would get in trouble when he would teach the Bible to families who could read. He would give them a Bible and have them read to him the word, then tell him what they thought it meant. Once he was reprimanded by the local bishop. "How dare you allow the common people to read and understand the Bible! Do you believe they can learn more than we can, and can teach their families better than we can? It is our job to interpret the word and instruct them as to how to live it out. They must never be able to teach themselves, or we will lose this control over the crowds, which will lead to chaos and ungodliness."

Andre kept teaching and growing the local people, and they came to love and respect him as the leader of their faith.

Father Andre assured Sister Anna that it would be all right, that the men had left, and the police would eventually capture and punish them. Andre knew who both groups were. He had kept an eye on the SOTH, used the underground tunnels, and kept in touch with his family in Jordan. They had established a support system for SOTH members whose faith made them targets in the countries that were Muslim majorities. He knew the Cleansing Group as well and was shocked to see them getting so close to the truth.

He had been contacted by Edgar through e-mail, something about his DNA marker making it plain he was a relative of a person healed by Jesus Christ. He never returned the e-mail and erased his digital footprint so as not to be connected to the SOTH movement in any way. Father Andre was a man of peace and service to his local Parish. He lived a simple, subdued life, one that could be called ordinary. He had watched as other priests had risen past him into the ranks of the important. He sometime thought if he could hold one of those positions, he could do some good for the glory of God. But then he would realize that living at that level of religiosity would lead him to embrace something more than a relationship with his savior. Andre would stay where he was, serving, healing, praying, and watching for the return of his savior.

SOTH underground facility

Edgar and his young brilliant apprentice, Jennifer, were busy testing the functionality of the new software. Edgar named it the Awareness Bug. It was designed to infect every computer platform connected to the Internet. It would be spread through e-mail software and take a week to be fully integrated into the world's systems. The plan was to "turn on" every phone, tablet, laptop, and desktop at the exact same time. Sarah of the SOTH leadership would begin to show the world the proof that the man, Jesus, was in reality the son of God and the savior of the world.

Top secret CIA facility, Annapolis, Maryland

Garret's father paced the floor of his tactical unit. "Where is my son, can somebody tell me where my son is?"

He had heard about the botched attempt at the church, and eyewitnesses told him the SOTH had taken his son away. Now he was both angry and fearful. He knew the SOTH had special powers, somehow turned on by the DNA aberration caused by the healing touch of Jesus Christ. He didn't believe this of course, but he couldn't deny their special powers handed down through the ages. It was a genetic mutation attributed to something, but not something spiritual.

He had long ago erased any interest in spiritual things. He followed his father, Garret Sr.'s, way while he was young, but found new interests in college, a small group of young scientists who had harnessed the power of the mind, and needed no God to help them. He was enticed by the ease with which he could "turn on" his mind power, subduing students and influencing professors as he wished. He graduated with a double major in business and psychology, married a fellow scientist member, and had one child. He named him after his father as he planned to raise him to represent everything his own father fought against.

There were times he regretted his ugly feelings for his father, but then the dark power would return, and he would embrace it with all of his soul. He was recruited by the CIA, and this fueled his love for power and control. He met every kind of person while serving, many who were like-minded in their pursuit for power and freedom from the civility of the world. While on assignment in Syria, he was introduced to a man who represented a group of leaders who needed a contact in the CIA to help them cover their tracks as they prepare the world for the next social evolution of the species. They were slowly building up a culture change, using religion, violence, terrorism, and the willing media to create a world in chaos, upheaval, and moral ignorance.

This would lead to a confused, wayward, subdued population they could manipulate and control for generations to come. Garret's father agreed to become the mole they needed. The next week, he set up a phony meeting with a terrorist and had the Cleansing Group, as they called themselves, stage an assassination of both he and the man he met with. The bomb wiped out half a block, killing many and injuring many more. There was no way to identify those closest to the blast, so Garret's father was listed as missing and lost in action. This freed him to stay connected to the CIA and pose as a CIA oversees handler needing a computer hacking team to help him track and eliminate terrorists. Enter Garret Barkley, a young talented computer hacker who had been with the CIA for several years. He was recruited, trained, and assigned a set of contacts to track and surveil. Garret never knew it was his father directing his every move.

SOTH underground facility

"Garret," Akifah asked, "do you know your father well?"

Garret sighed, "I knew him growing up, but he was always distant, busy, involved in secret things a son could never know about.

He encouraged me to explore my world, told me to look at all the world religions, political persuasions, and never be told by them how to live. I never felt I belonged to anything, and I felt alone most of the time growing up. I followed him into the CIA so I could be with him more. Soon after that, he was lost to a terrorist bombing. I have not had him in my life for a long while."

Akifah sighed, "That is a sad story, Garret, and I hear your heart breaking as you share it. I will pray for God to comfort and calm you as we work together for his purposes."

Garret was amazed by the change in Akifah. She was wanted by several countries, and her reputation as a cool headed killer for hire still made him cautious around her. "How have you reconciled your new faith with the one you grew up with, Akifah? They are very different faiths. Surely you will be shunned by your Muslim family and friends. What will you do once all this is over?"

"Oh my, Garret, don't you realize it was not an even exchange, one religion for another. My Muslim faith taught me to obey, submit, think in logical terms, and always, always punish a wrong with unmerciful justice. I was taught to hate, now I love, I was taught to be subservient, now I am a willing servant, I was taught to hate the infidels of the world, now I love the world as Jesus does, every person, like they are the last one on earth. I am free to pursue God now, Garett, free to enjoy an intimate relationship with the true God of my soul. No, it was far from an even exchange, and I am willing to pay whatever price God chooses in order to bring this message back to the people I love."

Garret said, "You may not get a warm reception, Akifah, in fact you may be risking your life to share your new faith."

Akifah smiled, "I have been used by the enemy to kill, torture, and destroy in the name of power and control. I have much to repay the world for my past, and risking my life to do good instead of risking it for what I have done these past years is not too much to ask."

Edgar and Jennifer began the process of loading the awareness software onto the Internet. Every time there was a keystroke using the awareness software, it would infect the other computer or smartphones on the other end. That device would in turn infect any devices it connected to as well. Every phone call, Facebook post, text tweet, snapchat etc., the bug would load and wait for the digital signal to be given.

They tested it with the hundred phones and tablets that were available to them from the SOTH team attached to the great revealing. The next day, they activated the software and sent a general message with photographs and video attached. It worked perfectly, and everybody received the message at the same time. Some got a text, others an e-mail, and others, a YouTube message. All of the world's technology was reliant on the other, and it was this web that would be accessed. Now it was time to get the rest of the artifacts safely to the rally point. This was the home stretch for the team, and they felt they would see it happen in the next few days.

Tehran, Iran

Omar couldn't figure it out. He had taken a team of assassins to Naples only to return two days later with no memory of why he had gone. His team had the same selective amnesia. What was it, why did he go there? He sat down at his desk, typed in his password, and checked his e-mail. There was an e-mail he had already read and not deleted yet. He casually glanced at it. It was from Akifah, his top operative in the middle east. "That's it!" he exclaimed! "Jonas, get in here, we have a mission to return to!"

CHAPTER 14

SOTH underground Facility

Garret typed in his password to the CIA mainframe, being careful to not violate any protocols that would expose him and cause a trace back to his location. Edgar assured him it could never happen with the software he had installed on the computers here. Edgar and his team had moved in and out of almost every major country's mainframes, connecting SOTH relatives to each other, and protecting them from the prying eyes of the Cleansing Group. Now he was in, and he immediately entered his old team's computers. He noticed that they had been dormant, like nobody was working on them. This confirmed his fear that the team had been disbanded after his faked abduction, and a new team would be organized to take their place.

Garret searched for his handler's e-mails, and traced them back to a firewall that he could not attempt to penetrate. He never knew their names, only that they had a list of people they wanted him to follow and report back to them about. Now, Garret realized that they were hunting SOTH members through him. Garret searched the mainframe for any hint that the CIA had a general set of instructions to hunt and collect SOTH members. It seemed that this operation was off the books, and there was no further activity pertaining to the SOTH in any other CIA database. Edgar sat down next to Garret and heaved a long sigh. "It never ends, does it?"

"I'm not sure what you mean, Edgar. What never ends?"

"The chase, the hunt, the never ending exchange of information for other information. We keep using each other, making certain we possess more information and hence more perceived power. Our lives revolve around this lie, Garret, the one that says if you just keep looking, you will find enough knowledge to help you find peace and fulfillment in this life."

"I used to think that way, Edgar, I used to believe that he who knew more controlled more. Instead, I spent the past three years of my life following and setting up innocent people like you for a group of corrupt and murderous kooks who believe the world could become a better place under their rule. It never ends, one dictator losing out to the next, all the while waiting for the next one to wipe them out and take over."

Edgar sighed again. "I know we are doing the right thing, exposing the world to our precious collection in order to convince them of the reality of Jesus Christ's love for them. Sometimes, I grow weary of the fight, the hiding, the things done in the name of Jesus that might not actually be of His making."

"Edgar, I believe that you are going to shock and awe the world into actually considering the truths of Christianity, and the implication of what a real, here and now God could mean to our world as a whole. People confronted with the truth will either fall to their knees in worship under the weight of that truth, run from it with all haste, or attempt to hide or destroy it with all their might."

Edgar wheeled his chair around and turned to go. "Have you had any success at getting to the bottom of who has been directing your actions these past three years?"

"No," Garret said, "but I think I know what has to be done. I have to go back to the CIA, be your eyes and ears next week, and the time following the revealing. It is the only way I can accurately identify my handlers and keep them off your trail."

"I have been thinking the same thing, Garret, and praying that God would confirm this direction if it was his. Let's talk to Sarah and the rest of the group and see what they think."

Askum, Ethiopia

Bohnna looked around to see if the area was clear of tourists and townsfolk. Aksum had been his family's home for generations, each priestly generation sworn to the safe keeping of the Ark of the

Covenant. An order of priests had protected this site since it was built. They guarded the Ark of the Covenant, as fantastic as that seemed.

Bohnna's family descended from Chander, the man who carried Jesus' cross. He had brought the message of the Jewish Messiah to Ethiopia, and eventually all of Africa would be impacted by the message of forgiveness, love, peace, and mercy. The chapel had long been investigated and no Ark of any kind had been found. The few tourists who ventured this deep into the country to see it were a little disappointed and frustrated, as some actually believed they would see the Ark itself. What the public, and all of Aksum didn't know, was that the Ark was there, tucked neatly beneath the structure, waiting for the right time to be shown to the world. Only the guards knew the opening, and each swore on their lives to only reveal it to their sons who would one day inherit the thankless and monotonous task of sitting at the chapel door, enduring the endless picture taking and silly questions thrown their direction until the evening came, and the area was shut down for the night.

Bohhna sent the message by phone and was immediately pinged back with the answer he was looking for. "East side entrance unlocked, bring the truck around now."

He returned to the truck and drove slowly so as to not attract attention. This was the same truck that came into the chapel area every evening to remove trash and clean the area for the next day. Nobody would expect one of the world's treasures to be taken out with the trash that evening. They would need at least four men to lift the Ark using the poles supplied for the task. The men would have to be careful not to touch the Ark at any time, as the last person to do that did not fare well. Bohhna asked two of his brothers to do the honors.

The chapel guard would make the fourth man. They backed the truck up to the east side entrance, entered the chapel, and stopped before falling into the six foot deep circle that took up most of the chapel floor. There was a set of stairs that switched back three times before reaching the bottom of the opening. The men moved quickly and located the Ark in its receptacle at the bottom of the staircase. It glowed with an otherworldliness, giving off energy that made their hair stand on end as they slid the poles into place. Each man felt an energy run through them, an energy that brought a surge of strength and sharpness of mind. They carried the Ark almost effortlessly, as if ten men were helping them. They slid the Ark in between the trash bins and covered it with trash and blankets. What a sight, The holy Ark of God placed amongst the waste of the world.

SOTH Underground Facility

Keener turned to Sarah and smiled. "We have been able to locate and will transport ten of the twelve pieces to the site by early next Friday."

"Good, Keener, thanks to God for our success there."

"Pieces of what?" Lindey asked, looking up from the table on which he was organizing scrolls and documents from thousands of years.

He was using his expertise in history to properly organize and document the written evidence that would be used at the great revealing. He had five assistants around him, all fluent in Greek and Arabic, more accomplished than he, but each humble in their service to God. Sarah turned to Lindey, "After Jesus was taken down from the cross, Nicodemus paid the Roman soldier to allow him to take the post beam of the cross with him. The Roman soldier didn't understand why he needed a piece of wood, but he was willing to take the old Jew's money. Nicodemus had the cross transported to his home where he had it cut into twelve equal pieces. After Jesus's resurrection and on the day before Pentecost, Nicodemus presented the twelve pieces to Jesus's disciples as they hid from the marauding temple police. 'Here is the cross our savior died on, see, even his blood remains on the wood, and it is soaked into every piece. I ask you to give these pieces to the twelve tribes, to those from the tribes who have given their lives to the Messiah. Have them protect and hide the pieces until God ordains they be revealed.'"

Nobody knew about DNA and blood back then, but the commitment was made, and the pieces were preserved for thousands of years. The wood seemed to have hardened, getting more solid and stable as the years went by. The protectors couldn't understand why the wood petrified like this, they believed it was God's work for some purpose they would never understand. Down through the centuries, the pieces were hidden, lost, reclaimed, taken again, even attempts were made to burn the evidence, but the flames bounced off the now hardened wood like water off a stone. Two pieces had been lost forever in the great cleansing of 275 AD, but the other ten were still intact and were now being transported to the place where DNA and blood samples would be taken, and tests would reveal that this was indeed the cross post that was used to execute Jesus of Nazareth. One more piece of evidence to show the world.

Garret finished his explanation of why he needed to go back to the states, back to the CIA. The room was silent for several minutes, and then Akifah said, "No, Garret, it has been too long, they will suspect you have been turned and will shut you up in a dark hole where you will never see the light of day."

Lindey agreed, "Garret, this can't be a good idea. Akifah is right, you will not be able to help us if you are locked up."

Sarah stood. "Friends, God has been clear in every step we have made or not made. I see valid reasons for and against this action. I believe we need to pray through the night and seek God's direction. Each of you go to your rooms, center your souls, and seek God's will on this decision. We will meet back here tomorrow at 7:00 a.m."

He was asleep as soon as his head hit the pillow. Lindey was back in the room, the room where he met the snake turned tiger. It was dark, and he could hear a sound somewhere in the distance. Suddenly, the room evaporated, and he was surrounded by creatures of great size. They glowed, giving off pulsating light that physically manifested and then dissipated into the air around them. He could hear a low hum, a rhythmic sound, like people chanting, but at a deeper, resonant level. The creatures were angelic in form and had human like anatomy, but weren't human, and much larger and pronounced in appearance. Their faces glowed and had a beauty deeper than any he had ever seen before. They were all looking forward, anticipating something or someone. Light began to shoot from each creature, piercing light, penetrating light. A beam shot right through him, and he anticipated being cut in two. He felt the light pass through, and felt the energy it left.

The light continued to move about, passing through him and the creatures around him. Then the song began. He couldn't understand the words, but the sound was physically impacting. He dropped to his knees, enveloped in the light and the music and the song. He knew it was what heaven must be, a place of powerful praise and worship with one goal in mind, with all attention and energy focused in one direction, in order to honor and worship the one creator, savior, sustainer, and Lord of all, Jesus. He fell flat on the floor, weeping, laughing, repenting, singing, completely absorbed into the beauty and intimacy of the moment.

Then he was awake. The dream did not leave him immediately. He could almost hear the last refrains of the song in his room as he began to fully gain consciousness. *What a powerful dream*, he thought. But knew this was no dream. This was a moment given by God to one of his children, a moment meant only for him and only for this time in his life. He wanted to return there, leave all this, return to the worship, to his dad, to Jesus. As the moment faded, Lindey knew that Garret had to go back, that it was part of God's plan, and that whatever happened, God would be there with them all.

Lindey was the last to make it to the conference room, carrying his coffee with him as he entered. Sarah remarked, "Dr. Batchleor, this is the second time you have entered our presence with the look of a man who had seen something special. Can you share what our Lord has told you?"

Lindey spoke, "It's still a little fuzzy, I'd like to keep it to myself for now as I need to process more before sharing all that happened. One thing I do know, we need Garret back at the CIA to cover for us as we make final preparations for the great revealing."

Akifah spoke up, "I too agree, there is too much we don't know about the people seeking to undermine us. Having a mole on the inside will give us an advantage we need at this time."

"I too was led to this decision last night," Sarah said. "It is clear that God wants Garret to serve him in this capacity. There is no guarantee of your safety, Garret, but there will be the guarantee of our prayers and God's presence as you go."

"Then it is settled," Garret said as he rose from his chair. "I'm already packed, and Edgar has been training me for the past two hours on how to use his software to safely communicate and pass information back to you all as I get it in real time. This mission will be essential to our success, and my need to understand who it is that has been pulling my strings these past years. Thanks for your prayers, they will be needed."

The group gathered around Garret and prayed with passion and love for their friend and brother in the Lord.

Omar exited the private plane in Naples, and immediately returned to the hotel he had just left the day before. He had just three agents with him this time. He needed to keep things on the quiet side this time. He would find Akifah, and either rescue or kill her when he found her.

Edgar's phone lit up with an emergency text. "Our friends have returned to Naples. It seems Omar can't get you off his mind Akifah."

Akifah looked shocked and afraid. Sarah walked over to her and embraced her saying, "God is with us, Akifah, and if God is with us, none can stand against us. Trust in God, and trust in our team of experts. He will not find us until we wish it."

CIA Facility, Annapolis, Maryland

Garett's father was encouraged by the news that his son had been spotted at the Naples airport. He had booked a flight for Dulles airport and would arrive the next morning. He wondered what had happened to his son, how had he escaped, and what had he learned about the SOTH that would be helpful. He was tracing a growing number of movements from the SOTH that had been identified and tracked by Garret and his team. They seemed to be moving in several directions, all to places of rural and non-commercial locations. He would contact Garret as soon as he landed and got his communication devises up and running. Time was running out, and he needed his son to step up and end this religious group of charlatans once and for all.

Garret made two calls on a public phone as soon as he arrived in Dulles airport. He called his grandfather to bring him up to speed, and he called the CIA office to let them know he had escaped and was coming in for a debriefing meeting. He would have to tell them something about his captivity and convince them that he was hot on the trail of finding the leadership of this religious group of fanatics. Garret would have to act like the Garret who worked for the CIA, the man who was cool, calculating, impersonal, and in charge. He did not feel in charge, and he asked God to empower and guide him on this mission. He asked for forgiveness for all the lies he was about to tell and for the people he would use in order to keep the SOTH members safe at all cost.

Garret was surprised at how quickly he was greeted at the airport. How had they known he was on this flight? That was a funny question as this had been his job for the past three years. One of his own team, George, came up to him and gave a bear hug that nearly cracked his ribs. "Gary, oh Gary, we're so glad you got out of there and back to us. When we saw you drop, we feared the worst."

"Just a sleeping drug, George, I woke up with a killer headache in an underground prison. They didn't harm me or even torture me. In fact, they didn't even ask me questions. One of the younger men got careless and turned his back on me while he was in the cell. I took him out, used his keys, and found my way up to the surface. I was in the outskirts of Naples and had no idea how I got there. I made it back to my hotel where they still had my things stored. I booked a flight this morning, and hear I am."

"That's great, boss, but you know we have to debrief you now, go into more detail, you know the drill."

Yes, Garret knew the drill, and he would play it perfectly in order to be released in a few days and do his best to protect the SOTH as they prepared for the big day.

CHAPTER 15

SOTH underground facility, Naples, Italy

Kreeger ended the call and let out a long sigh. "It's not happening fast enough, the collections are not happening fast enough."

Sarah turned from her computer and smiled at him. Keener had always been an overachiever, using his special talents to serve and preserve the history and safety of the SOTH along with Edgar's help. "Kreeger, God is guiding us, protecting us, and leading us to his perfect timing. We must proceed with haste, but maintain the margin of safety that protects the brave souls that are bringing their cherished treasures to us to show the world."

"I know, Sarah, but from where I sit, I have calculated the time it will take to gather, organize, prepare, and present all the artifacts coming in as no less than seven days. I don't know how we are going to keep our plans a secret from our enemies for that long."

"We must pray for God to blind the eyes of those who are against us," Sarah responded. "All we can do is all we can do, and the rest is up to God."

Lindey, Akifah, and three SOTH field agents waited as the plane landed and taxied to the hanger they were to meet at. The plane had a rear door for loading larger packages. The door opened, and a man with a skid loader drove up to it. Several loads later, Lindey could see the shape of a large square package with the name, "Naples Museum," stamped on it. That was the container they were looking for. Lindey presented his fake papers, along with ten crisp one thousand-dollar bills, and the transaction was complete. The agents loaded the box onto the delivery truck they drove in and left for the SOTH headquarters. Lindey was electric with excitement when he touched the container. This was it, the Ark, the one piece of history the Jewish nation had longed for all these years, and the one artifact the Christian faith revered almost as much. What would the world think when they saw this along with all the other proofs of the reality of the Christian faith?

Once they were on the road, Akifah could not contain herself. "I can't believe this is the real Ark, *the* Ark of the Covenant! We are sitting next to one of the greatest artifacts know to the world. It has been right where people said it was, but it was kept safe until this time. I wonder if it still possesses the power to destroy or bless as it was talked about in the Old Testament."

"How do you know so much about the Ark?" Lindey asked.

"My Muslim faith revered much of the Jewish Bible and believed the stories about the Ark. We saw this as a worldwide artifact, one that proved the power and wrath of the holy God. Now I see it as an example of a holy God inviting man to fellowship and come near."

Lindey smiled, and then ducked as the first bullet struck the windshield.

CIA Headquarters, Washington, DC

Garret arrived early for his debriefing. He was dressed in his best CIA suit, dark blue with a blue power tie. He observed that his team had already arrived, and were waiting for him with grim looks on every face. "Oh, God, give me favor, wisdom, and the right words to get through this and still be a free man."

The central figure in the room, someone he didn't know, began the interview. "Now, Mr. Barkley, let's start with the entry into the church…"

Backroad en route to SOTH facility

Akifah instinctively swerved the vehicle and tried to take out the passing vehicle. They responded by sending a hail of bullets into the side of the van as they passed by. "Is everybody okay?" Lindey yelled, as wind came ripping in the now open windows devoid of glass.

Nobody had been hurt in the first pass, but they knew it would not be the last. "Who is it, Akifah? Is it Omar? Has he found us?"

"No," Akifah yelled, "Omar would be more subtle, taking us out when we were stopped or unloading the Ark. This seems more desperate, unplanned."

They heard the roar of the engine behind them. It must be some sort of Hummer on steroids, because they had stopped, turned around, and caught up with the van, which was reaching speeds of over a hundred mph. Two of the agents who were in the back opened up on the Hummer as it approached at ramming speed. They took out both headlights, and managed to damage a tire before they saw the grenade launcher protruding from one of the rear windows. The Hummer swung wildly to the left, and the man with the launcher unleashed the grenade.

CIA Headquarters

Garret had been able to tell his story and convince the powers that he had escaped without compromising the CIA or government in any way. Further, he was able to share information that would prove useful to them in finding a group of terrorists in Naples who would be attempting to assassinate local leaders later that day. He even gave them the hotel where the terrorists were residing at, he even gave them a name, Omar.

Backroad en route to SOTH Facility

Akifah knew they had one chance, and she locked the wheels to the left as far as they would go, causing a hairpin spin that turned them in a 180-degree controlled spin. The grenade passed by them with three feet to spare. The explosion behind them was deafening, and they knew they only had seconds before the next one came at them. Akifah spun the van around and peeled away before the next shot came. They were shaken, but alive, and the Ark was still in their possession. Now to get to the safety of the SOTH headquarters. "Who was that?" Lindey yelled, still dealing with all the windows that had been blown out by the attack. "Who else would take such extreme actions to stop us?" Nobody had an answer, so they raced on in silence.

Lindey and his team arrived at the rendezvous point and waited two hours to be sure they had not been followed. They called the secure entrance and drove the next few miles with no incident. They arrived at the old barn, having passed no less than seven checkpoints they would never see. Akifah noticed three, but then she was a former world class assassin trained to see things others couldn't. They drove into the barn and waited for the lift. They felt a slight bounce as the lift started, but there was no sound of the mechanism at all. They lowered thirty feet into the earth as the floor of the barn slipped silently back into place. Lights came on, and all of the SOTH were there to see the Ark.

Lindey ran to the back of the van, saying, "We almost didn't make it, we were ambushed, but we made it out."

"Ambushed?" Sarah gasped. "Was it Omar, had the Cleansing Group found us at last?"

"I don't think it was Omar," Akifah said as she came around the back of the battered van. "This attack was more of an assault than a surgical strike. They were heavily armed, but not highly organized. I believe we are dealing with another adversary."

Edgar spoke, "Well, thanks to Garret, Omar had to leave Naples once he got wind of an attempt by an attack team to capture or kill a terrorist group with his name attached to it. They were last reported hightailing it to the border."

"Way to go, Garret!" Lindey cried, then he turned to the back of the van.

He opened the door, and they all looked at the large indescript container sitting there. There were several bullet holes in it, and they gasped thinking some had pierced the Ark. Lindey climbed into the van, and with several others, managed to push the container out onto the floor. There was an additional longer container, which contained the two poles used to carry the Ark when it was moved during the time in the dessert.

Each side of the container was carefully dismantled until the last wall fell away, and they were looking at the Ark of the Covenant. It was covered by an Ethiopian colored blanket, filled with pictures of the Ark and its journey from Israel to Aksum over three thousand years ago. Lindey slowly pulled off the covering, revealing the Ark. It was amazing, the wood looked like it had been cut earlier that week. The figures of the cherubim shining with an otherworldly glow.

Lindey slid the carrying polls through the gold rings designed to hold them. There it was again, a slight vibration, like static electricity pulsing through the poles and into his body. They picked up the Ark and carried it to a lab where they would perform tests designed to look inside without disturbing or touching the Ark in any way.

"Leave us for now, my friends," Sarah said. "My team has been waiting a lifetime for this moment. We will inform you of our progress tomorrow."

Lindey suddenly felt lightheaded and sat down hard on the floor. Edgar said, "Dr. Batchelor, I'm afraid all this excitement has exhausted you. Please go to the kitchen and have some nourishment before you go to bed. We will keep vigil over the Ark while you sleep."

"What else has come in since I was gone today?" Lindey asked. "Five more pieces of the cross have arrived, along with the plate used in the Passover supper. The cup is in transit, but we are fearful for the safety of the men who are bringing it to us. It seems there is a group of marauders who keep showing up at every checkpoint and border crossing, asking for the group that carried the cup of Jesus. It has created a stir, and they don't feel safe traveling the normal routes. We are praying for their safety and that God will guide them in their journey."

CIA Headquarters

Garret arrived the next day in his old office with his old team. He was back in the saddle, leading a team again, gaining access to all levels of security, and all in just one day. Surely God was with him, and he made his plans with faith and confidence.

"Have we reconnected my son to the grid?" Garret's father asked as he sat in his central office.

"Yes, sir, we have given him his old office and his old team. He is going back to work for us today."

"Excellent, perhaps it's time to introduce myself, get to know my son again, and see what damage that cursed group of people did to him. It was only a couple of days, but from what I've heard, they are adept at getting people to do their bidding and believe they are doing a service to God."

He hated the SOTH, hated what they stood for, how they played on the weaknesses of people, controlled them with their "gifts," and how they were going to "save the world" by sharing trinkets and pottery from ages ago. He would find out if they had gotten to Garret, turned him, and made him one of their own. He would have Garret lead him to the nest they cowered in, and he would wipe them out.

Somewhere on the border in southern Jordan

Sulaph looked through the night vision binoculars and surveyed the border crossing. They had literally felt the presence of Godly intervention no fewer than five times since they left their small town in Jordan to make the perilous trip to Italy. Sulaph was a SOTH relative of Bartimaeus, the man who called to Jesus from the road to be healed. He called Jesus, "Son of David," referring to the lineage of Jesus as the legitimate heir to the throne. Jesus called him over, and smiling asked him, "What do you want me to do?" Bartimaeus asked him to give him sight. Jesus healed him right there. The religious leaders told the crowds that Jesus could do this because he was getting help from Satan. Jesus responded by telling them that Satan casting out demons just didn't make sense, as Satan would be defeating himself.

Jesus said he was the one more powerful than Satan, and that the religious leaders should recognize God's power when they saw it. They scorned Jesus for saying this, making them look weak and irrelevant. They also felt threatened by the growing number of people Jesus was healing, seeing them as a root of faith that could grow and overshadow their own religious power.

The healed man became a Christ follower and stayed with the apostles once the synagogue expelled him for telling people it was Jesus that had healed them. The result of the healing for this man was the ability to see details and remember everything he saw for the rest of his life. Today we call it a photographic memory. Bartimaeus was amazed at what he could see and how far he could see. Unfortunately, people saw this as a demonic thing, not a God thing, so he had to keep his gift a secret, and use it only for times when he needed extended sight to keep him and his family safe from the marauding temple guards who now had permission to jail anyone claiming to have been healed by the carpenter turned rabbi.

He was happy to serve the apostles and Jesus when they celebrated Passover that fateful week of joy and sorrow. As he cleaned up the cups and plates, he remembered the ones Jesus used to serve communion, a new tradition that would come to represent all the pain and suffering Jesus would go through in the next few days. He kept the plate and cup, stored it in a safe place, passing it down to the first-born sons for generations to come.

The plate and cup got separated during the cleansing of 275 AD when a SOTH relative had to split them up in order to keep them safe. In 1150 AD, Templar Knights were given both in a move to preserve and sanctify them as the church grew in power and influence. One of the knights was a relative of the healed demoniac, and he used his unique gift to keep the cup and plate safe until he was killed in the Templar cleansing of 1307. Both the cup and plate were passed back to the SOTH and kept in hiding for the time called by God.

Now, Sulaph was responsible for the cup. Another SOTH family had possession of the plate and was on their way to Italy before the great revealing. Sulaph spoke to his team, "We must travel tonight, go around the border, and meet up with our contact in Saudi Arabia in forty-eight hours. We have a private plane waiting for us in Tabuk, a gift from one of our inside people in the government there. We can fly into Italy and be there days before the great revealing."

Sulaph's unique gift inherited from his relatives had to do with extended sight. He could look at anything, and be able to close his eyes, zooming in, or zooming out like a computer screen. If he had the chance to walk around a site, he could see it in three dimensions, and store it on the hard drive of his brain for future viewing. He could drive through a town, and remember every side street, every house, every car, and even some of the people driving them. This gift would be useful to many governments, some who would torture him and try to learn his secret. They would never understand how he got this ability, and they would probably kill him trying to find out.

He had been helpful to the SOTH in Jordan, giving directions to those looking to escape the death squads of Islam, who saw all Christ believers as infidels, worthy only of death. Now Sulaph was closing his eyes, seeing every inch of the border crossing, seeing the guards, their cars, the lights, zooming in to see the computer monitor in the guard house that showed the names of people who might want to cross the border illegally.

His whole team was on the list, with facial recognition pictures as well. This is how he escaped the Jordanian death squads and how he got them this far. Now, they would have to cross the border old school, like he had for years before when helping Christian families escape attack by crossing over the Jordon border into Israel. He scanned the border fences on both sides of the gate, closed his eyes, they opened them, seeing the best route around the guards. They had forty-eight hours before the plane left without them. God would guide them, this they believed with all their hearts.

CHAPTER 16

Garret settled into his work station and logged into the CIA mainframe. The familiar e-mail with the code words, "hacker heaven," told him he needed to log onto a secure site to receive the message from his mysterious handlers. This used to excite him, someone new to hunt, some new life to invade and surveil. Suddenly, he was over it, all of it. He knew he could never be happy here again. His eyes had been opened to a life with a third dimension to it, a spiritual dimension that made him feel more alive than any hunt could ever cause again. He opened the encrypted e-mail, and read it.

> Garret,
>
> I am happy that you are home in one piece. The CIA shrinks tell me you are in top condition and that your temporary capture did not affect your ability to continue your duties. I want to set up a meeting with you tomorrow morning. I will send directions later. Let's meet at 8:00 a.m. at the designated place. I look forward to answering some questions I'm sure you have been waiting to ask me.
>
> Phoenix

That was it. The person always signed e-mail as the Phoenix. He didn't even know if this person was male or female. Phoenix. Rising from the ashes? Someone who likes birds? Likes to fly? Whatever, he was going to meet with them tomorrow. He quickly moved to another site, using the software Edgar had given him. Once he loaded it into his laptop, it scrambled all GPS, satellite, Wi-Fi, Bluetooth, or any other hardware designed to receive and track e-mails and website activity. It was as if Edgar had studied their secret software and added a patch to disarm it in a way that would not be discovered.

He would log out after each e-mail, and the software would shut down before the next security sweep of the mainframe had a chance to intercept it. Garret e-mailed Edgar and let him know that he was in and was loading the seeker software into the mainframe tonight. This little bug would give legitimate data about non-existent places that would seem like safe houses for the SOTH or even a headquarters.

When the attack teams arrived, they would find themselves in an old ruin or deserted farm in the middle of nowhere. This allowed Garret to appear to be gleaning information they could use to track down the SOTH. Garret also let them know he was to meet with his handler tomorrow morning, something he never expected to happen. Edgar assured him that they were on schedule toward the great revealing and asked that Garret let him know of any intercept teams that may get assigned to Italy over the next few days. Garret agreed and signed off. "We are taking a great risk having him back at his old job," Kreeger said.

"Yes," Sarah agreed.

She had come to the kitchen for some coffee and a sandwich. They had been working on the Ark for four hours straight, using x-ray, CT scan, MRI, and even some top secret scanning device that one of their operatives had taken on his way out of a facility in England. "We are using everything we have to look into the Ark, but everything seems to bounce off the surface, leaving us with cloudy and unreadable data."

"We could just lift off the lid and take a look inside," Akifah said, walking into the kitchen looking for her own early morning snack.

"Yes, we could," Sarah answered, "but we aren't certain that would be a safe move."

"Indiana Jones?" Lindey spoke up.

"You're afraid something like what happened in the movie will happen to us?"

"Well, we have been careful not to touch it as the biblical reports showed that people died when they touched the Ark."

Lindey responded, "Yes, that is true, but there is no record of spirits coming out of the ark and killing people. I vote we hook a crane up and gently remove the lid."

On the border in Jordan

Sulaph gave the order and they moved with stealth to the eastern side of the fence, which was bristling with electricity and video cameras. Sulaph watched as the men cycled through the series of feeds for the many cameras they were watching. He was certain they had five to six minutes before the cycle was complete and the camera would expose them for the criminals they would certainly be shot as. One of his team had an ingenious way to bypass the electric fence without setting off the security system. He clipped a wire onto the fence and formed an arch four-feet high and wide. Once complete, he would connect the wire so a complete circuit would stay established even after they had made the cut and moved through. Sulaph looked ahead, closing his eyes and seeing more. "Can you see in the dark, Sulaph?" one of his team asked.

"Yes, but not as clear, I can use the ambient light, but it only works so far. I think I see snipers on the ridges in front of us. Unusual security for an outpost so out of the way. Yes, snipers, one each on the five ridges in front of us. Nothing to the north, so that is where we will go."

One of the team brought up fence clippers and went to work. The bypass worked perfectly, and in four minutes, they were through and had reconnected the cut fence to look intact to the camera, which was just coming on as they moved into the shadows.

SOTH facility, Naples, Italy

Jennifer called Edgar over to her workstation. She was wearing a frown. "What it is Jennifer, what do you see?"

Edgar knew that Jennifer could see code in every file she viewed. It was part of her special gift, but that was not that gift that was working at this moment. She pulled Edgar over to her workstation and whispered, "Garret is in trouble, and he is being set up to take the fall for the botched attempt to capture us. I sensed this in my prayer time this morning, and I've been asking God to confirm it to me. I can see Garret being taken away by his own people. He has to be warned!"

"Yes, Jennifer, we will contact him right now. Did God reveal a time or place where this will happen?" Jennifer closed her eyes and focused on the vision. "I see a garden, no a park, with many people, and it's near large buildings with columns and stairways in the front."

Edgar sent the encrypted e-mail to Garret and waited for the confirmation that he had received it. Edgar prayed and called the SOTH together to pray for Garret.

Crossing the border in Jordan

Sulaph crept along the rocky edges of the cliff, careful to keep their movements slow and steady. He knew the snipers would be using FLIR technology, and would see his team as a red glow in their sites. He kept his eagle eyes on the sniper positions to make sure they would not decide to make a sweep of the area and catch them exposed on the cliff face. They came to the end of the path and had to start the long repel down the face of the cliff into the darkness below.

Sulaph heard a faint sound in his ear, the signal that the transport van had reached the rendezvous site. They would wait no longer than one hour, which should be enough time if they didn't encounter resistance along the way. Sulaph came down first, made a sweep of the valley, and tugged twice to tell the team it was clear to come down. He saw that the valley opened up to the north, meaning they would have to back track west through the dessert once they cleared the valley walls. When the last team member was down, they began their journey to the van.

Sulaph brushed away what sounded like a bug whizzing by him until he saw the dirt explode in front of him. He collapsed to the ground as another round came whizzing by. The team instinctively dropped into the shadows, and the sniper halted the attack. He wasn't very good, which was a blessing to the team. Sulaph closed his eyes and brought up the sight of the sniper on this hill just as he saw him before their decent. He must have started a sweep just as they dropped off the rope. There he was, leaning over a stone, trying to get a fix on them. Sulaph pulled out his own sniper rifle, a 300 Winchester Magnum he had been given by an English sniper whose life he had saved with his extended site.

Now, Sulaph was the hunter. He did not relish this job, he was a Christ follower, and did not enjoy taking a life. He moved into position, looked through the scope and took the shot. Normally a sniper would need a partner calling out wind speed, curvature of the earth, and humidity factors that would affect the shot from this distance. Sulaph could see all of this in a moment and dropped the man before he could get the next shot off. Now they had to move quickly. The rest of the snipers would get suspicious when their teammate did not respond to the next check in. They had five miles and fifty-two minutes to arrive before the van left.

Washington, DC

Garret was confused and uncertain. He read the e-mail several times, trying to believe the unbelievable. Edgar had told him what Jennifer had seen, and he knew it had to do with the meeting he was going to be at this morning. It was 1:30 a.m., and he had about five hours of sleep before he would have to get ready to be at the meeting place by 8:00 a.m. His handler had chosen a city park, right downtown in DC, where the United States Capitol building was. He could see the building with its large columns and wide stairways leading up to the entrance. Just like Jennifer said. Now, what would he do? He had no back up, nobody to help him if he did get into trouble at the park. Who could he call here in DC? Who could he trust?

Crossing into Saudi Arabia

Sulaph picked the shortest route through the dessert, paralleling the road, looking for the off road where the van would be parked. He strained his eyes, trying to pick up on the furthest place he could see, which was about one mile out due to the lack of light and the heat coming off the sand. There, there it was, black and concealed to all eyes but his. "I see it men, I see the van."

They hurried their pace and arrived with two minutes to spare. This van would take them straight to Tabuk Airport. From there, they would fly to Cairo, refuel, and take the long flight to Italy. The final stages of the journey were in their sights, so to say.

Washington, DC

Cody came awake on the third ring. He heard someone on the other line, but they weren't talking. He knew this was a test, with a code word needed from him to confirm he was the person on the phone. "Geesh, is this a crank call or do I need a lawyer?"

"Hello, this is Garret, Garret Barkley."

There was a hesitation on the other end, and Cody said, "I'm sorry, I don't know anybody by that name, please don't call this number again. I have had you blocked."

Garret knew that was the code to wait until he could get to a second burn phone the government didn't know about. Three minutes later, his phone vibrated to life.

"Cody, is that you?"

"Yes, Garret it's me. What is going on?"

"I need your help, Cody, I think I'm in too deep, I think I've been set up."

"Who is setting you up? I thought you just returned from being captured and escaping from some terrorist group in Italy."

Garret mused, "So they are calling it a terrorist group, are they?"

Cody yawned, "What do you need? I'm here."

Reception room, SOTH facility

Sarah had returned to the Ark and had taken Lindey's suggestion to open the Ark. A small overhead crane stopped over the Ark, and Lindey attached the padded connector to each side of the lid, being careful to only touch the lid with the connectors, never his hand. He felt that soft, static release just like before, but it was nothing to be afraid of. No, he wasn't afraid at all. In fact, he was calm, collected, and a little euphoric. Somehow, he knew it was all right to lift the lid himself. "No, Lindey, don't do it!" Sarah shouted, but it was too late.

Lindey had connected the crane, lifted the lid a little, and touched the sides of the lid, gently lifting the lid off the Ark. Inside was exactly what the Bible had said—the tablets from Moses and the staff that had budded. Lindey was in awe and just stared at the artifacts for a few moments. Sarah called him back to the present by asking, "What do you see, Lindey, are they there, are they complete?"

"Yes," Lindey sighed, and the whole team let out a collective breath of praises to God.

The most holy and revered artifact of the world was sitting in their lab, and God had blessed them indeed. Lindey spoke softly, "Someone should contact our Ethiopian friends, and let them know the good news. Be careful to share only the code words they need to hear to know the Ark has arrived safely."

Lindey reached into the Ark and pulled out the first tablet. It was the last five commandments, etched by what looked like a diamond laser. The words were clear and sharp. He pulled the second one out, careful to lay them on the padded blankets designed to hold them safely and ensure they would not be disturbed until the great revealing had begun.

He pulled off is protective gloves and stepped away. Now the experts would step in, taking pictures, measurements, documenting every inch of each stone. This was a miraculous moment for the world, and soon, the world would share in this truth. Akifah spoke through tears, "It is real, it is all real, I mean I believed it was real before, but now my belief is confirmed."

Sarah smiled, "Yes, child, it is real, as are the other artifacts we are collecting and organizing. The world will soon see that Jesus, is real, that God's love is real, that all of it is real. Millions will come to the savior, and we will be free to share our true history with the world."

Garret used his burn phone to call his grandfather. It was 7:00 a.m., and he wanted to talk to him one more time just in case. "Grandpa, this is Garret."

"Garret, oh, son, we are so glad to hear from you. Where have you been? We have been praying day and night for your safety and protection."

Garret smiled, "Well, so far, those prayers are being answered, so thanks. I have a big meeting in an hour, one that may take me away again for a while, I don't know for sure. I wanted to hear your voice once more, and tell you how happy I am that you and Grandma are in my life. You are a part of me, and now that I know my real family history, I am committed to live up to that legacy any way I can."

"Garret, son, you sound ominous, like something bad is about to happen."

"No, Grandpa, if everything goes well, in four days, something glorious is going to happen. I love you both, and thank God for you."

They prayed on the phone, and Garret hung up, dropped the phone in the toilet, and prepared for his meeting.

National mall, Washington, DC

Cody had collected the surveillance equipment Garret had asked for and was sitting in the make shift command center, which was a rental van parked near the park. Garret placed the tiny hearing device in his ear, did a sound check with Cody, and exited the van. "Let me know when you see his people closing in. We will only have one shot at this, and we will need to be perfect with the timing."

Cody responded, "I have three cameras placed so that I will see them coming from a hundred yards."

"Be sure to take lots of pictures and video, and make sure our conversation is recorded."

"Don't worry, Garret," Cody yawned, "I think I know what I'm doing."

"Thanks, Cody, I didn't know who I could trust with this."

Cody yawned again, "Get out of here before I start crying and hug you!"

Garret moved to the bench he was instructed to sit on. He thought he saw at least six operatives moving in and out of the park. Cody checked in, "I see six operatives moving just outside of your position. I will let you know when they start to converge."

Now, Garret had to wait. He felt exposed, vulnerable, and betrayed by his team. He knew that if he survived this meeting, he would never be able to go back to the CIA. He felt more that saw a man come up from behind him, standing just outside of his peripheral vision. Cody called to the earpiece, "Where did that guy come from? Do you see him right behind you!"

Garret remained calm, and called out in his best relaxed tone, "Have a seat, sir, best seat in the park."

The man came around the front of the bench, the sun shining over his shoulder, blinding Garret for a moment. "Thank you, son, I believe I will have a seat."

Garret knew that voice; he had heard it before.

"Garret, I think we have a lot to talk about."

"Yes, we do," Garret said. "I'm glad you're okay, Dad. I look forward to catching up."

CHAPTER 17

San Lorenzo Maggiore church, Naples, Italy

Father Andre found the stone to push that would release the floor covering the stairs leading to the underground tunnels. He carried a large flashlight and a satchel. He made his way through the tunnels he knew so well. How many had found shelter and protection down here from those who hated them for their choice to follow the Son of God. He also knew the SOTH patrolled and protected these tunnels, so he knew when to turn off the light and blend into the darkness. He was looking for the tunnel that led to the SOTH headquarters, or meeting place, he didn't know what to call it. He had followed them several times to memorize the way, but the tunnels branched off in many directions, making it difficult to remember the way. He noticed a red blinking light in one of the ceiling corners and stopped dead in his tracks. He could go in quiet or go in with style. He chose style, turned on the light, and strode into the eye of the camera.

"Breach alert, tunnel 23, we have a breach in tunnel 23." The announcement came over the communications speakers, and the whole place jumped into action.

Ten field agents grabbed their guns and lights, donning night vision goggles as well. The blast wall was sealed behind them making it impossible to get inside short of a small nuclear device detonated at the door entrance.

Father Andre shined the light around as he made his way down the tunnel. He stopped when he heard the footsteps of the agents coming at him. "I am unarmed, and I bring a gift to my brothers and sisters of the SOTH family."

He dropped to his knees, put his hands above his head, and repeated his greeting. Edgar watched as the lead agent came around the tunnel with his helmet cam on. He said, "I know that man, that is the Father from the church where we staged Garret's abduction. I met him several times as we scoped out the church for our operation."

Sarah told the agents to treat the Father with respect, no cuffs, no blinders, as it was obvious he knew them and knew where they were located.

Father Andre smiled as he entered the meeting room where the SOTH leadership were located. They had searched him and found only a satchel with small round parchment holder. "My fellow believers, I am Father Andre of the San Lorenzo Maggiore church. I am a SOTH survivor and have been watching and praying for you all these years. Now that you are planning to share the riches of our faith, I thought it time to partner with you and share the gift our Lord gave my family so many years ago. Please, allow me to open the tube."

Sarah handed him the tube and asked, "How have you known about us all this time? Do others know? Are we compromised?"

"No, not at all, my child, your secret has been safe all these years. The Lord has made it clear as to your presence, and only recently had I know what you were going to do with the artifacts you've been collecting."

"But how did you know about that?" Lindey gasped.

"God speaks, my son, he speaks in my spirit, in his word, and in dreams." He winked at Lindey when he said the last line and smiled as if they were sharing a delightful secret. He continued, "I had been the blessed protector of a document that will aid you in your efforts to waken the world to the reality of God and his love for them. Please, have one of your interpreters read this document."

He pulled out a pair of gloves from the tube, and then he pulled out the document. It was amazingly preserved, as if it had been written that week. Lindey listened as the interpreter read the ancient script. On it was a statement by, no this must be wrong, it was a statement about Jesus signed and dated by the governor of Jerusalem, Pontius Pilate!

National Mall, Washington, DC

Garret turned to his father as he sat down next to him. He knew the clock had started ticking, and that his time would run out fast. Cody would let him know when they started to close in. Garret's father began, "Have you known it was me for a while, Garret? You don't seem surprised."

Garret sighed, "I guess. I always hoped I would find you, and over the past three years, I was suspicious when some of the e-mails you sent contained phrases I had only heard you say when you were with us. It was only an inkling, like an itch at the back of my brain, but now that you are here, everything makes sense."

His father got right to the point, "What happened in Naples, Garret? How did you allow yourself to be captured by such amateurs?"

"I wouldn't call them amateurs, they were quite prepared and quite effective in taking out our team without killing anyone."

"They are amateurs, Garret, and I think they got to you somehow. I think it is time to bring you in for more questions, with the aid of some of our best interrogation medications."

It broke Garret's heart to hear his dad talk to him like a common spy, one that needed to be broken. He remembered how distant he was while he was young and how he practically disappeared after becoming an agent.

"Dad, what happened, why are you so adamant against these people? What have they done to you?"

Garret's father grimaced, "They aren't people, son, they are mutants, dangerous creatures with delusions of grandeur, thinking they can convince the world that God exists, and that he actually loves mankind with some sort of celestial affection."

Garret heard the signal from Cody, two beeps, meaning he had two minutes until he was overrun.

"Dad, I don't understand why you allowed me to pursue every world religion but Christianity, and why you told me lies about my family so I wouldn't meet them and understand who I was and where I came from?"

Garret's father spit out the next sentences with vitriol and hatred. "Has the old man been telling you stories, Garret, unbelievable lies about our heritage? I believed those at one time, until I learned about real power and control. They don't come from submission to some power hungry being bent on controlling mankind. Real power comes from within, from our own power, knowledge, from our mind."

Garret heard one beep and knew he had to move. He stood up, and when his father tried to stop him, he sprayed an aerosol filled with anesthesia, and guided his father back down to the bench. Now, he could see the operatives coming, just fifty yards away. He took ten steps onto the concrete path and came to his escape. The manhole cover had been loosened and had yellow cones around it, like it was being used by maintenance workers. That someone was Cody, and his finger was on a red button. Garret slid into the cones, dropped into the hole, and slid the manhole cover over just as the agents reached his father.

Cody pressed the button, and a small, blinding light raced around the cover where it sat in place. The agents came to the cover and tried to open it, but they withdrew their hands in pain as the cover was hot and solidly in place. It has somehow been sealed in the time Garret entered to the time they approached it. They would find every cover within a quarter mile sealed in the same way. Garret knew they were coming, he had planned his escape. Who was helping him, and what was his plan?

The interpreter read the document again, slowly, so all could hear, "This Jesus of Galilee has been brought to me by the Jewish leaders with accusations of violating their religious law and planning an uprising against Rome. I have interviewed him and find nothing that would lead me to believe he is anything more than a deranged prophet who believes he is the son of God. The leaders have stirred up a riot, and I have given them a choice between two prisoners, Jesus and the criminal, Barabbas. They have chosen Barabbas to be freed. I write this memo into the official books that I find no guilt I this man, and I wash my hands of the proceedings that will take place later today. I hereby condemn this man to death by crucifixion.

Signed, and sealed by my own hand, Pontius Pilate, Roman governor of the Jerusalem province."

Artifacts room, SOTH facility

Lindey was the first to speak, "Is this real, Andre, is this really the handwriting of Pilate?"

Andre replied, "This document has been handed down to my family since the days of Christ. A Christ follower in the house of Pilate was able to collect this and several other documents as he was leaving the house to follow the way. He was hoping to give them to the disciples for safekeeping, but was delayed when the temple guards came looking to arrest any disciple claiming to be a Christ follower. He decided to keep them and pass them down, hoping to save some history of that fateful day. After Jesus' resurrection, any document referring to the event was taken out of the official archives and burned. Only Josephus and a few others reported the crucifixion and resurrection as really happening. The Jewish leaders paid off the Roman soldiers to tell the story that Jesus's body had been stolen by the disciples on the day after the Sabbath."

Lindey turned to the interpreters and asked them to use every tool they had to prove this document was what Father Andre claimed it was. Sarah moved to the Father, took his hand, and raised it to her forehead, saying, "Father Andre, forgive us for our rough treatment of you, we welcome you to our family, and praise God for your blessed gift to us."

Father Andre embraced her saying, "It is I who am blessed by this group of faithful believers who desire so much for the world to know the love of the savior."

The next morning found another artifact being delivered. This time, it was Sulaph who made the call and found the entrance to the SOTH stronghold. He presented the cup and thanked them for the privilege of being part of the great revealing. Lindey took the cup gently in his hands. It was a simple cup, made from clay and fired to a hard gloss. It would have been the type of cup used in the upper room of a citizen of Jerusalem.

Carbon dating would reveal its age, and it would be added to the collection for the great revealing. Jesus touched so many common day items, things that had no value until they were attributed to Jesus. The cup was one more ordinary thing made extraordinary by the touch of the master's hand. Sulaph was welcomed and encouraged to stay for the revealing. "Thank you for that honor, but I think I must get back to my home in Jordan, where I can respond to the questions and interest that will be generated when your revealing rocks the world."

Many hugs and thanks were traded, and he was off to his home to prepare for the great revealing.

Washington, DC

Garret thanked Cody for all his help. "No worries, Garret," Cody yawned. "Now I can finally get some sleep."

Garret climbed into the rental car and headed south, to the one place he knew his father would never come to, his home.

Garret's father awoke in his office, lying on his leather couch in the corner of the room. As he came around, he knew he had been played by his son. He was enraged and stewed all morning. Finally, he called in his team leader. "I know where he is going, back to his grandparents' arms, back to his useless new faith, and with him all the information we need about what the SOTH have planned. Round up the team, and fuel up the plane. We will get there before him and give him a proper greeting."

Computer command center, SOTH facility

Jennifer smiled as she sat back on her chair. She was tracing the infection rate of the awareness software they had planted on the Internet. It was 70 percent saturated, meaning most of the Internet had "shared" the bug with their Internet friends.

Soon, the entire net would be available to them for the great revealing. Lindey was frantic with his job, logging, categorizing, taking pictures, doing tests, and stopping every once in a while to be astounded at the plethora of ancient documents, artifacts and proof of the life, death, and resurrection of Jesus Christ. The SOTH had been faithful to God in all they had preserved. Many had wanted to share their gifts and their treasures with the world, but they knew they would be snuffed out by any number of groups who were after them.

The adversary that hurt the most was the church. The Christian faith grew under the blessing of Constantine where Christianity became the legal faith of the empire. As the religion of faith grew in size and power, men began to assert their own ideas of faith, religion, and how to live out that faith day to day. The church became the authority for the masses, who, being uneducated and poor, looked with trust and respect on the ornate priests and leaders of the local and worldwide church. When word of the sect of the healed reached the church's ears, the response was swift and condemning.

Anyone with a history of association with this group called the SOTH would be thrown out of the church and possibly punished. SOTH families serving in the church were asked to leave, and some disappeared never to be heard from again. Rumors spread that there was a group of religious zealots who believed the SOTH to be Satan's tool to seduce and destroy the church using their special gifts passed down from the people healed by Jesus. They were responsible for the lost lives and missing people that were being reported. The local townspeople fell for this false reporting and became the eyes and ears of the local church. The SOTH went into hiding and have stayed there until today.

Garret kept the radio off on his ten-hour drive to his grandfather's home. How disappointed he was in his father. He was shocked to see it was really him, but somehow he knew that his father had lived and was keeping up with him. He tried to understand why his father had abandoned his faith, and he replayed his father's words about where true power came from. Garret knew now that true power came not from the biggest or toughest or strongest or fastest, but from the man who could put his faith squarely in the living God expressed in Jesus Christ. Plugging into that power would make a man ready for anything. He had activated the wormhole software Edgar had given him, and it was now infecting the entire CIA mainframe. He would be able to enter his father's site and follow his every move.

Garret Sr. had just locked up and turned the downstairs lights off when he thought he heard a slight sound, like a pebble glancing off a piece of glass. He stood still and heard nothing more, so he went upstairs. At the top of the stairs, he heard his son's voice, "Well, Daddy, it seems you have been reaching out to the relatives. That was the wrong thing to do. Dragging Garret into this will only bring more pain to you all."

"I didn't drag him in, son," Garret Sr. said, slowly climbing the stairs and looking for his wife.

"Looking for your wife? She's resting comfortably, waiting for you to lie down next to her."

"He contacted me, son, he claimed he was directed by God, what could I do with him showing up unannounced?"

"You should have thrown him out and acted like the demented man I described you as being. Now you've filled his head with your nonsense, and he is on some kind of religious mission for this group of misfits you call the SOTH."

"Arthur, son, please listen to what you are saying, where has this anger come from? Can't you see it is a false power that you worship, a false hope in yourself put there by the very enemy himself!"

"There are no personal devils, Dad, just the ones you dream up. Now, go upstairs, be with your wife, and let me do my job."

Artifacts room, SOTH facility

Akifah entered the room where Lindey was working. "Well, Professor, tell me how we are doing?"

"Doing?" Lindey sighed as he stepped away from the table full of delicate and precious relics from the time of Christ.

"I'm standing in a room full of things that speak to the very reality of Christianity, its rich history, its miraculous growth, and how real the Bible really is. Nothing could have made me happier than to be a part of this."

Akifah smiled, "I too am touched to see so many proofs of the faith I now embrace. All this coming from people who were healed by Jesus, and passed their DNA down all these years. What will the world do with all of this proof and truth? Embrace it? Reject it? Try to destroy it? Maybe all of the above I fear."

Lindey walked around the table until he was in front of Akifah. "Akifah, your newfound faith is a blessing to watch. You have really been filled with God's presence, and you are eternally bound to Him forever. My faith was on hold until I was roped into this crazy plot. I guess I have been finding my peace with God, understanding more of His perfect power and will, which are surrounded by His perfect and powerful love. I know now that my father's time had come, and he used that time to lead many closer to the Lord. Suffering separates our true beliefs from our religious beliefs, leaving a pure faith that is attractive and influential. Yes, I too think that we will have to endure many reactions to the truth we are about to release to the world. We can't predict what will happen, we can only obey God's calling and watch what happens."

Edgar shouted into the room, calling out to everyone, "Come, you all have to see this!"

Warrior, Alabama

Garret pulled up to three blocks away from where his grandfather lived in and shut off the car. He knew that his father would have likely flown to here in order to lay a trap for him. He pulled up his laptop and typed in the commands to boot up the surveillance cameras in the house. His grandfather had initially rejected the idea of the cameras, but Garret convinced him that they would be useful if he needed to know what was going on before coming home. His discreet placement of the cameras, and his father's arrogance ensured that none would be found while doing their job. Garret used the heat sensitive setting to see where all the players were. Five were inside, with another five outside. Garret knew he was beat, so he packed up and pulled away. He had the CIA mainframe under his watchful eye, and now, he could track his father as well. It was time to inform the

SOTH of what he had learned, and find out how the operation was progressing.

Planning room, SOTH facility

Edgar led them to the large meeting room, where they watched a TV reporter talking about an explosion that had occurred in downtown London. The Fox and Hound pub had been totally destroyed with multiple deaths and injuries. Lindey didn't understand, and he asked what they were watching. Sarah spoke in hushed tones, "This is the headquarters of the SOTH initiative in England. All of our people were there preparing to assist with the great revealing. Someone just wiped them out. We have to find out who is responsible, and we need to know if there are any other places that have been compromised. We are so close, and we can't afford any exposure until we are ready for it. Edgar, it is time to engage the defense system for our brave SOTH operatives across the world." Edgar agreed and called Jennifer over to the large desktop system. It was time to really show the world what Edgar could do with a software code and keyboard.

Chapter 18

Garret drove back to DC, called Cody, and asked to bunk with him for a couple of days. He really wanted to go back to Italy and help with the preparations, but he knew he was needed here. He opened the laptop, typed in the correct codes, and smiled as he was looking at the CIA mainframe desktop on his laptop. He typed in the keywords for his father's group and waited to be connected. He found very little on the group, and no mention of his father as he was still marked as MIA. He activated the wormhole software and was soon connecting to his father's e-mails, being able to backtrack into his father's laptop and trace him by pinging the location GPS the laptop used to know its location and road system reports. "Now, where are you, Dad?" Garret asked as he started the search sequence.

The next few days were filled with artifacts delivered, cataloged, prepared, and marveled at. The rest of the cross post arrived, all ten pieces intact. The plate arrived by way of Naples airport, delivered by a SOTH member from Switzerland. Rose Stein traced her family back to Jerusalem where her relative served as a gardener for the man who hosted the disciples and Jesus at the last supper. He and Justin's family had agreed to split up the artifacts to ensure some would make it through the centuries to be revealed at the correct time. Now, Rose was beaming as she presented the plate to Lindey and cried as she looked around at the growing testimony to Jesus her Lord.

Jennifer called Edgar over to the screen she was looking at intensely. "Somebody has found our worm, Edgar, look."

Edgar engaged the trace software, which was able to do a back trace on a computer without the person running it knowing. There it was, a special boring software, designed to recognize and destroy and software it deemed dangerous or infiltrating. Edgar flew through the keys, like a man possessed. Jennifer stepped back and gave him room, marveling at his abilities. Soon. Edgar sat back, breathed a long sigh, and reported, "The software is safe, I just gave the hacker a false program to chew on. He will think he defeated the person trying to hack his mainframe, but with every keystroke, he will be spreading the awareness software to every computer on that mainframe."

"Which mainframe did the attack come from?" Jennifer asked.

Edgar smiled, "China, of course, they are always first to recognize a hacker."

San Lorenzo Maggiore Church, Naples, Italy

Andre returned to his home, secure in the belief that the great revealing would soon happen, and many millions would be coming to faith in Jesus Christ. He didn't see the gun before it was too late.

Garret's father had put a team together to go back to Naples and find the liar of the filthy SOTH leaders. He gave strict instructions that no person is to survive this attack. No prisoners, no questions, and no survivors. They traced their path to the church, and did an extensive search of the area, looking for underground passages, assuming that was the only way they could have escaped. The leader of the team took another agent with him to the church parish where they waited for the priest to return from his trip visiting the sick and poor.

They would have to risk questioning him to find out more about the church and its architecture. They had been waiting in the dark for thirty minutes when they heard the key turn in the old house lock. Father Andre entered and went straight to the back of the house. The lead agent intercepted him at the kitchen with a blow to the head intended to disorient, not kill. The priest fell hard to the floor and laid there looking dead. In a matter of minutes, he shook his head, sat up, and leaned against the hallway wall. The agent would not enjoy his actions tonight, this was a priest, and he was a church going man back home in the states. He chose the faster acting drug in order to spare the father more pain and suffering than he needed to cause.

Cyber café, Washington, DC

Garret read the e-mail giving instructions to the field team assigned to Italy. They were already there, and he had to warn his friends to be ready for an attack. He pinged Edgar, which allowed him to call Garret on a non-traceable phone he gave him before he left.

"Edgar," Garret talked fast and furious. "There is a hit team coming back to Naples to find you all. They have been in Naples since yesterday, I only just found out. I don't know where they will go, but you are all in danger."

Edgar replied, "Relax. Garret, nobody has found this place for seventy years, and I don't think your crack team will do any better, unless—"

"Unless what?" Garret said.

"Unless they find somebody to question, like Father Andre."

Edgar barely got the sentence out as he was flying over the keys again, searching for the location of Father Andre. "How could you know where he is?" Jennifer asked.

"By activating the tracking beacon I gave him to wear around his neck at all times. It looks like an ornate cross, but it is a new type of device that allows me to know where he is and listen in to anything sound within thirty feet of him."

Edgar brought up the beacon and used an overlay map to confirm that he was at his Parrish home, right where they expected him to be. What he heard next stopped him in his tracks. "Father, we know you were involved in the capture of one of our agents right here in this church earlier this week. Tell us the location of where he was imprisoned, and we will leave immediately."

"No, no, I don't know anything, just that my church was shot up by what the police called a gang related event. Why is the room spinning? I feel so light headed."

"That would be the truth drug we injected, Father. It will soon take over and allow me to know what you are hiding here at your church."

Edgar and all around him swung into action. A field team of ten men were on the run to the church. Edgar phoned the police and reported strange activity at the parish house, and all of them prayed for Father Andre.

Lindey was dreaming again. This time it was Akifah who was with him. She was moving toward a door that was half open with light spilling out from the cracks in the door. This was the same door he saw in another dream, the door where a man was killed and he was warned about going to the cave that night. He reached out to stop Akifah, but he could not reach her. He cried out, but she seemed to not know he was there. She reached the door, pushed it open. and was immediately shot. She fell back grasping at her chest in disbelief. A red spot formed on her shirt as she collapsed on the front porch. The door was closed, and Lindey woke with a start. What was this dream? Was Akifah going to die? Was he going to save her? When would he know what to do? "Oh, God, show me the meaning of this dream, and guide me to protect your new child, Akifah, from any harm that may try to come at her."

Then he got up, showered, got some coffee in the kitchen, and ran right into a flurry of activity. Father Andre in trouble?

Father Andre could feel the drug taking affect. He was not a field agent, and did not know how to resist the effects of this truth drug. Gradually, he would relax, feel good, and start talking. It was then that the knock on the door happened. One of the agents signaled that it was two local officers asking for Father Andre to open the door. The lead agent cursed and told his men to exit the building In the rear and leave the man for now. How did he get caught like this? Somebody must be watching them. He bolted out the back door as he heard the sounds of the front door being kicked in.

Edgar breathed a sigh of relief as he heard the police breaking in and coming to the father's rescue. Father Andre told them, "It was a group of youngsters looking for money to buy drugs. They took my cash and some items, but they did not harm me."

The police took down his statement, which was difficult as he struggled to tell lies while under the influence of the drugs. Once they left, he heard a knock on the back door, and was relieved to see five SOTH agents looking worried and ready for a fight. They would bring the father back to the headquarters until after the great revealing was over.

Everyone at the SOTH headquarters breathed a sigh of relief as they heard the police coming in and taking over the situation. They rejoiced when the SOTH field team arrived and escorted Father Andre back to his new home for the next few days. Lindey found Akifah and told her his dream. He knew she was tough enough to hear it, and knowing might just save her life. "Lindey, trust in God, he will guide and protect us on our mission."

Lindey sighed, "I know, Akifah, but I don't want to lose anyone again. I know suffering comes this side of heaven, but I am stuck on this side of heaven, and I couldn't stand to lose another brother or sister to the evil that is the Cleansing Group."

"We must serve where we are placed, Lindey," Sarah said as she entered the kitchen that had become Lindey's unofficial meeting place. "God can't show us the end of every decision, only he knows the plans he has for us. Our challenge is to discern and obey his will for us as we understand it."

Lindey smiled, remembering how his father would say such wisdom is so little words. Yes, that was the challenge, faith was the belief that whatever was going on now would make good sense some-time later, even if not until heaven.

Washington, DC

Garret took a chance and called his grandfather. He watched on one of the cameras as Garret Sr. came to the phone in the hall-way. "Hello, Barkley resident," he said as he looked to the camera. He made a signal that the phone had been bugged and people were listening. Garret spoke anyway, knowing that the scrambler system in his phone could never be traced. "I know they are listening, I just wanted to make sure they didn't hurt you."

"Son, it was your father, he would never hurt us. He gave us a knock out drug though, and your grandmother is still sleeping."

Garret fought to control his anger, "I'm not going to quit you know, and I won't let you hurt my new family, do you hear me?" He turned his voice back to his grandfather. "I'll let you know what happens soon, Grandfather. Keep the faith, and trust in God"

"That will be an easy order to obey," he said, and Garret hung up.

Garret's father cursed and asked, "Did anybody trace that call?"

"No, sir, he hung up five seconds before we got a lock. All we know is that he is back in the DC area."

"Then put out a net for him and find him!" he screamed.

It was almost as if Garret had a mole in the CIA to keep him informed and one step ahead. Maybe not a mole, but a worm. He ordered his cyber team to go through the mainframe circuit board by circuit board to find any hardware or software that had be attached to the mainframe. They warned it could take days to do a complete sweep, but Garret's father ordered it anyway. He must find the bug, and use it against Garret.

The next call from Garret was to Edgar. "Is everything okay, Edgar? You sound busy."

"Yes, we are," Edgar replied. "We have just rescued the father, and shut down a cyber attack from China. Things are heating up, but we are managing with God's help. How is it in the states?"

Garret replied, "Well, you know, family can be tough sometimes, lack of communication and all that."

"I know what you mean," Edgar said, "Please be careful, and let us know what they are trying to do. We are so close to telling the world all that we have to tell. Keep in touch, and keep your head down over there." Garret smiled and hung up.

Keeping his head down was easy, staying out of the clutches of the CIA would be harder. The leader of the team in Naples watched as the police left the parish home. He noticed an officer placed at the front door and a police car parked outside. They would not get another chance tonight, so the team stood down and retired for the evening. They would come back and finish their time with the good father.

Lindey began to prepare the rooms for the great revealing. One room held larger objects like the ark, the cross post assembled, and then tables of artifacts attributed to Jesus and his time on earth. Another room was filled with written proofs, all of them stretched out carefully and protected behind sealed glass. The reports from Pilate would prove to be the most interesting, but so would letters sent between the apostles, the written diary of one of the people who saw Jesus after his resurrection, and several documents from Constantine making Christianity the religion of the world at the time. So much missing history made Lindey wonder how much more was out there.

He was standing near the Ark when he felt something. It was like a whisper, as if he could barely hear that someone was trying to speak, but didn't have enough volume to be heard. He moved out of the room into the hallway, looking to duck into one of the many rooms off the main corridor. He found one and dashed in, closing the door, and started listening.

The CIA field team was regrouping at their hotel when the call came in. Arthur Barkley was on the line, asking to speak to the team leader. "Yes, sir, we had to retreat when the local police showed up. Yes, sir, I agree. It's like somebody knows our next moves and is blocking us at every turn. Yes, sir, I know finding the SOTH head-quarters is the top priority. We will revisit the father tonight and complete the mission as stated." The team leader hung up, and called his team together. "All right gentlemen, we need a plan to find this headquarters, and we need to find it in the next twenty-four hours. I want every contingency plotted out. so we won't be caught with our shorts down next time. Stay off all technology until we are certain we have not been digitally compromised. All communication will be in person. Turn off your cell phones, remove the batteries, and store them in the lead lined techno storage unit we use to contain enemy technology. From now on, we are off the grid."

Sarah turned her attention to Edgar and Jennifer who were huddled around a main screen at the end of the conference room. "Edgar, how is it going?"

"Swimmingly. Sarah, absolutely swimmingly." Edgar replied, eyes glued to the screen as his fingers flew over the keyboard. "The software is now in every mainframe in the world and making its way into the rural and less populated places as well. This is amazing when you think of all the algorithms and back door bugs you have to get through to make something like this work. We are certain that five billion out of eight billion people will see the initial reveal, with most of the rest seeing the recast that will happen four hours later, once the media have made it the top news story to follow."

Jennifer explained, "No computer or device infected will be able to be turned off or switched to something else once the software is activated. It will play out the presentation over and over, unless the person can remove the battery, smash the screen, or hide the device under a pillow."

They all smiled at the tremendous things that had happened to make this coming day one to be remembered for the ages to come. Jesus Christ would once again be exposed to and confirmed to the world.

Lindey called Sarah to his quarters. She came in and sat down. "Sarah, I know you have experience in supernatural things, a lot more than I have, that's for sure."

"We all seek the same supernatural God, Lindey, you have as much access to him as I do."

"I know," Lindey said. "It's just that I don't know how to process things that I've been experiencing. The dreams have been so frequent and so lifelike. I feel like I'm actually living them out. Then a little while ago, I was standing near the Ark when I heard a small whisper. I found a quiet place and just listened. Sarah, I think I heard communication from God, an angel, or something supernatural."

"Go on," Sarah said, leaning in and communicating warmth and support.

Chapter 19

Cyber cafe, Washington, DC

Garret had to be careful not to expose himself digitally in any way. The CIA had many ways to locate a target, which was just what he had become to them, a target. He left his friend's home to find a cyber café where he could get back to work helping Edgar, Sarah, Lindey, and the rest prepare and be safe for the great revealing. A couple blocks away, he found what he was looking for—fast Wi-Fi, private worksites, and a quick exit if needed. He logged on to the CIA mainframe, crossed his fingers, then uncrossed them, prayed to God for protection, and typed in the activation code for the software. Instantly, he saw the e-mails streaming from his father's account. They seemed to be going for the digital crumbs Edgar was feeding them. Soon, they would launch an attack at an abandoned shoe factory in Dublin.

The CIA field team in Naples was getting anxious, they wanted to go back and finish the interrogation with the priest. "He's not there, boss, we used heat seeking video and found nothing but the cat inside," the team leader wondered out loud. "Where are you, father, and who is hiding you?"

He sent a crew to the church to give it one more try, but it too had been locked up tight with local police surveillance actively protecting it from the "gangs" who had recently marred it with their violence. They would have to find another way to discover the hiding place of the SOTH.

Garret was glad to see Edgar using his version of skype. "Are you keeping safe, staying off the grid like I showed you?" Edgar asked.

"Yes, Edgar, you'd think I'd know how to do a thing like that!"

Edgar smiled, "I loaded a new software into the phone you're using, so you'll need to turn it off and back on to install it. It will enable us to track you at all times and graphically see the terrain or buildings you are near."

"I'm glad you're on my side, Edgar," Garret laughed as he reset his phone.

Edgar said, "We are ready to activate the awareness software, we are just waiting on Professor Batchelor to finalize the artifacts for us to properly display and present them."

"I'm praying for you all. Edgar, God willing we will be reunited soon."

Edgar looked over his shoulder as if someone was talking to him in urgent tones. "I have to go, Garret, it's another hacker trying to lock down our software before we activate it. God be with you."

The screen went blank as his phone chirped that it had rebooted. What was going on, and who was on to them?

Edgar turned to the main screen. Jennifer was working to identify the hacker trying to back trace them. If he succeeded, they would be found out in a matter of hours. Edgar flew into action, creating one false ping after another, sending his IPS into servers as far away as Tokyo.

"There, now this hacker will be hot on the trail of a high school girl in a cyber café in Akito, Japan. I hope they have frequent flyer miles!"

Everybody sighed and relaxed for a moment. It was getting harder and harder to deflect major attacks like this. Hackers would likely be sharing information on what they were finding, so the team needed to move up their plans to tomorrow.

Sarah went down to the rooms Lindey was working in. "Lindey," she said, "how is it going?"

"We are close to being ready, Sarah, it's amazing what we have here. I can't wait to see what happens when the world sees this!"

"We need to hurry, Lindey, Edgar just deflected another cyber attack, but we won't be able to stop all the ones that will be coming soon. We need to active the awareness software and share out story with the world tomorrow at 10:00 a.m. eastern United States time."

"Wow, this is really happening," Lindey said.

"Yes," Akifah said as she stepped into the room. "I want to be of help running point near the entrance of our home away from home. I know what a hit team would be doing, how they will approach, and where they will be vulnerable. I want to lead the team that will defend us if such an attack should occur."

They all agreed, and Akifah went off to organize her team.

Keener came into the room, looking tired and ashen. "What is it, Keener? You look shocked."

Sarah said as she sat down next to him, "It's the Scotland team, they have disappeared, all of them, gone. I can't reach anyone on the team. My friends, my family, all gone."

Sarah responded in gentle tones, "Maybe they are in hiding, Keener, safe, but off the grid for now. Do you have a process for contacting them when they have to go into hiding?"

Keener looked up, a spec of hope in his eyes. "Yes, Sarah, in the event of a breach in security, they were to disappear and contact me in analog ways only. There is a phone number to an old analog phone we carry that can be used to contact them. Do we have such a phone here?"

The Stay Inn, Washington, DC

Garret said a prayer for the team and made his way to the hotel. He was paying cash provided by his friend, Cody, who had withdrawn 5000.00 for him to disappear with. Garret checked in, but didn't notice that the front desk man looked a little too young and polished for such a position. He was too focused on thinking about the fact that the reveal was actually going to happen tomorrow. What would the world think? How would people respond? How would the media spin it? Just the Ark alone would turn eyes in every nation. Then all of the artifacts, the nails, the cross post, the documents from Pilate, and so many more. People would have to believe, wouldn't they? Garret slipped the key card in the door, but it wouldn't open. He tried it again, and the door remained locked. Inside, a team of three agents waited with a stun gun, tape, and cuffs. They would not let their man get away once he was in the room. Garret was frustrated by the key card and started back to the elevator. His phone chirped, and he took it out of his pocket. Two words made his eyes go wide. 'Run, Now!'

Edgar had been following Garret as he walked back to his hotel. He could see the buildings and surroundings as the GPS software gave him details of every building Garret passed by. Edgar did a quick check of the hotel and noticed some changes in the security system. Certain cameras were turned off at certain floors and walkways. His antenna went up when he activated the hotel cameras outside and saw a large, black van, signature CIA. Edgar immediately found Garret's room and deactivated his key card remotely. He then typed two words and hit send.

Once outside the hotel, Garret called Edgar. "What is going on, Edgar? We just talked."

"Garret, the CIA knows where you are, they may be waiting in your room. I deactivated your key card just in case. Can you find a safe place to crash until I can so some reconnoitering?"

"Yes, I have a friend."

"Stop right there, Garret, your phone may be compromised. Shut it down, take out the battery, and leave it somewhere right now. Contact me by cyber café later tonight."

Garret did what Edgar said and found a small café in the suburbs of DC. He sat there, regaining his composure. *So this is what all those targets felt as we hunted them*, he thought to himself. To be on the run, never certain if your cover was working, or if the next person you met had a stun gun and cuffs. He knew there were bad people out there, people who deserved this kind of treatment. How many "bad people" had he hunted who were just people who got in the way, knew too much, or made waves in places they weren't supposed to. It was always about control and power. No matter who was in power politically, there were always enough boogey men on either side to hunt and take care of.

Where did it all end? he thought. His new faith was showing him the amazing peace, joy, strength, and courage that a relationship with God could bring a person. Seeing life through the eyes of love and mercy allowed him to seek peace with all people, no matter what they believed. *Unconditional love,* that was it! He had received this love and was now charged with applying it to everyone he met. That would be hard with his dad, and others who saw that kind of love as a weakness to be exploited. Maybe you needed to be wise in applying this love to all people. After all, there was a new enemy he was fighting, and people, like his father, had unwittingly given themselves to this dark power. He added wisdom to the new gifts God was showing him. He would be loving, but shrewd as he looked to survive in this new life.

Hotel, Naples, Italy

"There it is, sir, we can see it clearly on the x-ray picture." Eric, the team leader, had asked the CIA strike team to search the basement one more time, this time with a mobile x-ray machine that could look under floors for any passage that would allow them to escape a hotel that was totally surrounded and locked down. "It's clear there is something down there, a passage of some sort. Now, we need to find the opening in the basement."

"Go," Eric said, "Find that opening if you have to tear the floor apart!"

Keener came back with the good news that the Scotland team had escaped with no fatalities. He was able to contact them using the analog phone system. Coverage was spotty, but he was able to confirm that they had been attacked, but thanks to Edgar's security software, they could see the attack coming and make their get away just minutes before the building was obliterated. Who was discovering the SOTH hideouts, and why were they attacking with such force? Was it CIA, Cleansing Group, or a combination? Why would somebody so hate them for bringing truth to the world? But he already knew the answer.

Truth was in the eye of the beholder, and their truth about Jesus was seen by others as a threat to their way of living. Keener knew that there would always be a group of God haters who would be seeking them and disrupting their lives. This is why Jesus said, "In this world, you will have trouble, but be of good cheer because I have overcome the world." It was this promise for daily overcoming that gave them all hope, peace, courage, and purpose.

Outside the SOTH facility, Naples, Italy

Akifah had coordinated defensive activities to be taken in the underground passages as well as the road approaching the above ground entrance. They knew they were safe behind the blast doors, but they didn't want to spend the rest of their days there. The plan was to capture, not kill, any team and then introduce them to Edgar. They would be dropped off far from Naples and wonder why they were there. Cameras were placed two miles away in the passages, and false passages were created to mislead and confuse those who had never been down there. Trip wires were placed miles away from the above ground entrance with stun grenades positioned to render a truckload unconscious in a moment. They felt they had a good chance at stopping the attacks before people got killed. They prayed for protection and placed their defenses for the night.

Basement of the Digorno hotel, Naples, Italy

Eric got the call he was waiting for. They had found an old door with a new lock on it in one of the older sections of the basement. They blew the door hinges and stepped inside. They were greeted with what looked like old cobblestone passages going every direction under the newer city above. This was where the targets had fled to. It would be easy to find them now. Eric transmitted the good news to his handlers, stocked up on ammunition, and led his team into the passages.

It seemed like any passage would pass for an exit point, so Eric had to send teams of two into each branch to track it as a possible exit. This would cost him hours he didn't have, but it was the only way to cover ground and eliminate each passage way. Then he got the idea of using an overlay map of Naples on his tablet to aid him in determining some sort of general direction. He had a hunch that these passages may pass under the church they were staking out.

Looking at the roads leading from the hotel to the church, he was able to eliminate passages as he moved on toward the church. In under an hour, they were standing under the church. It was then that Jennifer sent the alarm to the defense team. They could see the CIA strike team on their monitors. The cameras under the church were hidden behind brick and lead, making them undetectable to even a trained technician.

Akifah acknowledged that the first attack was coming from underground. They would mislead, confuse, and attempt to neutralize the strike team before they got within a mile of the headquarters. This was different for Akifah. Before finding God for real this time, it would have been easy to set up booby traps that would kill every person on the team in a matter of seconds. Life was more precious to her now, even an enemy's life. She looked forward to the fight, but was happy it would not lead to deaths this time.

Eric pulled his team together. "We should assume that we have already been discovered, so the element of surprise is gone. We must also assume that there will be resistance as we press on. Everybody needs to lock and load. Our orders are no prisoners, no interrogations, and no loose ends. Now, let's do our jobs and finish what we started here."

"They will be cautious from now on," Edgar said as he switched on the series of screens that displayed the many cameras installed on the passages. "We have closed off the passages leading to this site and will try to lead them away into the passages that end in open fields and old buildings. Hopefully, they will see this as an escape route only, not a passage to a large hidden operations site."

"We should also prepare for an above ground assault just in case," Akifah said as she came into the technology hub of the center.

"Good idea, Akifah," Sarah said. "Position two-thirds of your team in the passages, and one-third to the road leading to our entrance. Let us pray for God to be with us, and pray for no life to be lost for all involved."

They prayed together, and each went to their assignments.

Lindey stepped back and took it all in. Two large rooms, filled to capacity with relics, paintings, written materials, art, and many

Christ-centered artifacts. This had to be the greatest collection of early Christian and Jewish religious pieces the world would ever see. He was proud to be a part of it, and proud to know his father was cheering him on. He now knew all of it was true, his father's faith, God's love, and his limited knowledge comforted by the boundless love and holiness of the father, God, working to reclaim his creation even now.

On the run in Washington, DC

Garret typed in the password that would connect him to Edgar half a world away. "Good, Garret, you are safe," Edgar said as he activated a scrambler software that would bounce this connection around hundreds of IP addresses.

"I'm not sure how they found me, I took all the precautions I used to employ in reversed when hunting for the CIA."

Edgar replied, "We aren't sure of all the new technology that is out there. But I'm betting it was facial recognition software that found you. DC has over twenty thousand cameras up and running, and every face is run through a program with thousands of people they are searching for. You are in the central part of that digital net. Be careful as you walk the streets."

"How can I help, Edgar? I feel like I'm on the sidelines biding time."

"Do you still have a back door to the CIA mainframe?" Edgar asked.

"Yes, I do," Garret responded.

Edgar smiled on camera, "Great. Maybe You can help us by trying to meddle with the CIA strike team that is here in Naples and are now in the passages below the church."

"What?" Garret yelled, then looked around as others in the cyber café looked at him as a librarian would. He lowered his voice. "How could that happen?"

Edgar smiled again, "Relax, Garret, we have planned for this kind of event for a long time. Akifah is heading up defense teams for both entry points. We have blocked our passages and will lead them away on a glorious goose chase."

Garret wasn't feeling as optimistic as Edgar. "They won't stop, Edgar, they will keep coming until they find you."

"God is with us, Garret, we are anxious for nothing. We will do all we can and trust the rest to our Father. I believe we will still be able to bring the great revealing to the world tomorrow as planned. After that, we will trust God."

Edgar signed off, and Garret got up to leave. Wasn't that the same guy who walked by a couple of minutes ago?

In the tunnels under Naples, Italy

Eric knew he was being watched. Why weren't they attacking? He knew his team was well trained and would be able to overcome any untrained group of Bible study idiots. He came to a split in the passage, a three-way split. He looked at the ground to see which path was well used. The ground was smooth and un tracked, as if somebody had swept every passage clean of footprints. He looked at this map overlay and narrowed it down to two of the three passages. He also kept an eye on his compass in case he was being led in a circular direction. He wondered out loud, "Where are you, people? Can't you just surrender and end this now?"

CHAPTER 20

Akifah led the team into the passages, now familiar with the path they were on. They carried a rake looking device that would use gentle puffs of air to disturb the dirt floor, making it seem that there hadn't been anybody through this way for years. They were using a tablet that was connected to all the cameras in the underground passages, and she could see the team making their advance. Three in one passage way, three in the other, both heading away from the passage to their facility. The leader seemed to have some sort of tablet in his hands as well, and he was looking at it often. "Edgar, this is Akifah. I have a visitor who needs to see things less clearly on his tablet."

"No problem, Akifah, I have identified the person and should start confusing him with our jamming system. It will take you offline as well, so turn off all your devices now, and use the analog phone in case you need something." Akifah acknowledged and let her team know what to expect. They turned off their devices and waited for the word.

Eric's team was plunged into total darkness. His tablet, their headlamps, even their targeting devices were off line. Eric told everybody to freeze, calling them to switch to battery flashlights as backup light. His tablet was fried, never to be activated again. He was impressed by their ability to activate a small pulsed wave that would fry their technology but not kill them.

Lindey reported to Sarah that everything was ready for the next day. He had called the video team to do a walk through to make sure they were able to cover all the major pieces in the ten minutes they felt they would have before they would be shut down across the world. He was in awe of all of the treasures, items that man had forgotten but would soon be reminded of. So many would have to consider the claims of Jesus and decide if they would follow the Lord of Life or stay in the darkness. He prayed that the truth would cut across all religions and cultures, all man-made faiths and traditions, and open the hearts of millions to the love, mercy, grace, and forgiveness of God through Jesus Christ.

Warrior, Alabama

Garret arrived at his grandparents' house sometime around 7:00 a.m. He knew the great reveal would happen in three hours, and he wanted to be with his family for the event. He was risking capture from his father, but it was worth the risk to be with them for this historic revealing. He called his grandfather while on the road, and he assured Garret that all surveillance had left, as if they were ordered to cease and move out. Garret was happy about that and pulled right into the driveway, greeted by them both as he got out of the car. Nobody saw the drone high in the air, capturing every move and transmitting it back to his father.

Underground tunnels, Naples, Italy

Eric used his flashlight to gather his team together. "Listen, they know where we are and are able to confuse our technology and knock it out. We need to retreat and bring back heavier assets if we are going to find them and stop whatever they have planned. Our superiors tell us this terrorist group has the means to tear Naples off the map, and they intend to do it very soon. All we can do is rearm and come at this in a different way. Let's go for now."

They gathered their equipment and started back through the passages they had marked on their way in. Edgar, Jennifer, and the team all raised a thankful praise to God for what they knew was only a temporary victory. "You better get topside and be ready for an assault from the road," Edgar told Akifah as she returned to base. "Be sure nobody can get through your defenses before the reveal is finished."

"Yes, Edgar," Akifah said, "I will make sure they get a rude awakening if they try to come down that road."

Warrior, Alabama

Garret set up his laptop and went to work. The first thing he noticed when he entered his father's computer through the software hack was that he wasn't where he was supposed to be. He also noticed that communications between the strike team in Naples and his father had stopped for now. The last contact spoke about a retreat due to low level pulse waves knocking out their equipment. Garret smiled as he imagined Edger pressing the pulse wave button with a big grin on his weathered face. There, he final got a fix on his dad's laptop. It was moving quickly high overhead. A jet, he was in a jet. Garret exploded the map to see the entire east coast. He watched as the red blip of the laptop crossed Charlotte, North Carolina, on approach to…uh oh, time for him to leave, and now! Garret packed up, kissed his grandparents goodbye, and slipped into the darkness. His father would once again be just a little too late.

Garret's analog phone chirped the old sound of the early cell phones. He read the text, which read, "This is Cody, they are looking for you in Alabama, you need to disappear now." Garret was impressed that Cody was able to use his mainframe hack as well. He texted back, "Just found out. On my way to a safe place to watch the party." He meant that he was going to find a place to be plugged in when the great reveal happened. This was it, the final countdown to what would surely be one of the most memorable days in history.

It was around 2:00 a.m. when Lindey fell into his bed. He was asleep in a moment.

Now he is standing, waiting, but waiting for who, or what? The place he is in is dark but feels safe. He sees a window and walks over to it. The window overlooks a city busy with life. People are moving along streets, sidewalks, and shops. Everybody is moving with purpose, heads down, not looking around. They seem possessed with their purpose, which seems to be to keep moving. He soon notices that they are making a huge circle around the city, moving away from the center of town, then branching out to the outskirts, only to return on a different road to the center area he looked out on. He also sees people waiting on the sides, looking for a chance to step into the crowd and begin their circular journey. Why were they doing this? What was the purpose? Couldn't they see the homes and shops just waiting for them to stop in at?

"This is their curse," he heard as a young bearded man came up behind him.

He was dressed plainly, but looked like he had just stepped out of a local clothes store. "They never stop, never look up, and never take time to see where they are going or where they have been."

He spoke softly but with a stricken passion reserved for somebody much older. "Who are they?" Lindey asked the man he knew was Jesus.

Lindey knew he was dreaming and speaking with Jesus. "They are those who worship man-made faith, religion, and activities made from man's broken imagination. They learn the rules, march in lockstep, and the enemy bows their heads so they can't see their deception. They keep running on the same path year after year. Sometimes, a person will stop, look up, and begin to understand. Then they are bumped into submission and move along with the crowd again."

"How can this be?" I asked. "Can't you just yell out, get their attention, and make them change their direction?"

"I never make a person do anything they don't want to do, never. Remember that, Lindey, I never make somebody do something they don't already want to do. I love them too much to coerce their allegiance and love. I know the ones who will turn, take the risk, and plunge headlong into a love affair with me. They will break from the crowd, and travel on the less travelled roads that lead to me. I will embrace them all, and welcome them into eternal life with me."

"But there are so many who look like they are missing the light you offer," I said.

"Don't worry, Lindey, I can see them all, love them all, and want to save them all. This is my gift to you, my dear son, my love for my people. Don't allow the world to beat you up and steal your joy again, never let that happen again."

"I won't, Jesus, I plan to stay connected to you daily, no matter what the cost is."

Jesus smiled, put his hand on Lindey's shoulder, and said, "Great, now get up and fight the good fight. Remember, you have some new tools to wage war against the enemy."

Akifah was waiting behind a large boulder that overlooked the valley. She could see the road for miles and felt secure in knowing she would defend the new family she had been blessed with. She missed her family back home, the ones she knew before she began her dark journey into power and self control. She was always proud of her self control, her ability to take the steps necessary to accomplish anything she thought to do. Now she relished the idea of total release, letting go, and trusting in a power so much more able to direct her life that she would ever be. She still had purpose, and goals, like protecting the SOTH and this road.

The difference was she found herself asking for help along the way. She spoke out loud to God all the time, even to the stares of the people around her. She was so dependent on her new relationship that she couldn't think of spending more than a few minutes away from thinking or praying to God. This was completely different from her old religion, something she did religiously, but with no heart and certainly no soul involved. Rote memory, doing the same thing, saying the same thing over and over. There was a kind of safety in the predictable, but it created a shallowness and emptiness she could never shake until now. This new life she was living was the way God intended for all his creation. Then she heard the sound of the drone overhead.

Edgar and Jennifer positioned themselves in front of two large monitors. They could see all the main cities of the world lit up with the awareness software. They had thwarted three more direct attacks to the software, and many more were happening in the background, but they were taken care of by the defender software within the awareness software.

Edgar said, "We are going to begin the countdown Jennifer, please bring up the activation software now." Jennifer keyed in the commands and the launch software was set at sixty minutes.

"We will activate the software in one hour, then three minutes later, we will begin the live video feed. Are you ready, Sarah, to tell the world what we have here?"

Sarah smiled, "I haven't slept all night spending time in prayer and outlining what I think God wants me to say. I know I only have ten minutes, but the world will be changed by what we do in that moment."

"I know what I'm going to say," Lindey spoke as he strode into the room, "I'm going to remind them all that it is love that has done this, love that did it so many years ago at the cross, and love that will continue to make the difference we could never make without it."

"Well said, Lindey, well said," Akifah broke in using the radio where she was perched looking over the safety of the group.

Sarah spoke up into the microphone, "Akifah, I have a feeling that strike team will be back soon, please be careful, and make sure they can't find their way here."

"Yes, Sarah, we are ready for an attack on both positions now. Whoever tries to stop this will wake up with a headache for the next few weeks." She looked for the direction she heard the drone, but it seemed to veer away from her position. Was this the CIA, or another adversary?

Garret found a small town down the road that had a McDonald's. *Good coffee and free Internet, my what a great nation we are*, he thought to himself. We had learned to expect much and live with much these past twenty years. If we needed something, technology would produce it for us. We had created over a thousand cable stations to entertain and engage us, as well as the thousands of video games and apps that took up the majority of our lives in vain and sometimes self-focused ways that rivaled idolatry. What if it all stopped, like some predicted when the solar storms were growing in strength. What if we woke up, and all we had to look at was each other and our deep need to be?

Garret looked around the restaurant, watching as people, young and old, bent their heads toward the technology they so dearly cherished. Soon, they would see a flash, a blank screen, then a message that would rock their world. Please, God, open the hearts of the world to you and your great love for them. I pray for my father, that even he would take a second look at the love and peace you offer. It was 9:30 a.m.;—almost show time.

Akifah saw a glint in her binoculars, a faint but definite glint of a drone high in the air. She radioed her team and check with the observer at the intersection of this road and the paved road five miles away. He reported no movements, and they all waited. Akifah had lined the road with shape charges designed to emit a small but powerful EMP. This would shut down all technology and transportation vehicles. Then there would be a loud percussion sound that would render all targets immobile and unconscious. Her team had special headgear to wear when the charges were released. This was the way they could render a strike team innocuous without harming one of them. They would be collected and transported to underground facilities where Edgar would have some time with them.

Edgar watched as the awareness software countdown continued. Sarah and Lindey had already gathered in the rooms they would be videoed in. Sarah was praying for God to give her the words that would open people's hearts and souls to his invitation. She knew this was what they had all been planning on for so long. God had empowered and protected them until now. She believed they would complete their mission and see millions come to the love of God found in his son, Jesus. Edgar signaled that the software was minutes away from activation. This was it, the moment they had all worked so hard for, sacrificed for, and for some even died for. The awareness software would capture the attention of the world, and the ten-minute presentation would be played over again millions of times until the whole world knew how loved they were by their creator. Edgar pressed the enter key, and the world changed forever.

See book two in the SOTH series to continue the story of redemption and challenges the team will face as the awareness software is activated and the world sees the artifacts, relics, and written proofs of the Christian faith. There are many twists and surprises that will leave you entertained and intrigued. Thank you for enjoying this book.

ABOUT THE AUTHOR

Dean Brior is a lifelong fan of good Christian fiction. He combines his own life experiences and current cultural issues to connect with readers across various cultures and beliefs. He has been involved in mentoring men, serving as an FCA state director, and teaching at the churches he has attended. One word to describe Dean is "enthusiastic." He celebrates life daily with his childhood love and friend, Nancy Brior. He is blessed with his daughter, Promise; her husband, Ron; and their two adorable children, RIV and Myles; as well as his son, Jesse. Dean's hope is that people will be drawn in by the storyline and will be challenged to look at their relationship with God in a new light.

CPSIA information can be obtained
at www.ICGtesting.com
Printed in the USA
FSHW010635130221
78467FS

9 781644 719732